This is a work of fiction. Simila events are entirely coincidental

THE ARTISAN

First edition. August 17, 2020.

Copyright © 2020 M K Farrar.

Written by M K Farrar.

Chapter One

The scrape of movement came from somewhere in the flat. Kerry Norris sat up in bed, her heart a heavy thud, vibrating through her chest. She'd been in a deep sleep only moments before, but something had woken her, fast and sudden.

Had it been a dream? Or a nightmare? Was that the reason she'd burst from sleep with her pulse thumping and her breathing short and shallow?

She froze, straining to hear, but struggling over the rush of blood in her ears and the hammering of her heartbeat. Why was she so certain a noise had woken her? It was probably just her cat, Merlin. She glanced down to the spot at the foot of her bed where the cat normally curled up at night to discover it empty.

It had taken an additional deposit to convince her landlord to let her have a cat. He hadn't wanted pets, and since she was on the first floor, she didn't have any access to outside space either. All she had was a tiny balcony that was barely big enough to fit one of those bistro-style table and chairs onto, but at least Merlin had a little bit of outside space. He could sunbathe in a patch of sunshine when the weather was warmer, though she'd had to put chicken wire across the railings to ensure he didn't decide to jump through.

Kerry blinked in the darkness, the only light from the LED clock and the gap in the bedroom door. She lived alone and never slept with it fully closed. Merlin needed access to the litter tray, and there was no way she'd have it in here.

If something had woken her, it was most likely only the cat deciding it was time for breakfast and knocking something off the kitchen sideboard in protest.

Kerry tried to focus on the digital clock. With her eyes still blurry from sleep, the red light was a haze before the numbers took shape.

02:11.

"Ugh, Merlin," she groaned. "It's nowhere near breakfast."

Damned cat.

A scrape came from the direction of the single room that served as both her kitchen and living space. The London flat was tiny, and she paid an insane amount of rent each month, but it was worth it not to have to share with any flatmates. She knew the cat wasn't going to allow her to get back to sleep until she'd put some food in his bowl. At least after he'd eaten, there might be a chance he'd curl back up on the bed.

Reluctantly, she threw off the soft covers, still warm from her body heat, and stood. She shivered, her shoulders shuddering. It was January and too cold to be creeping around her flat at two in the morning. The central heating would come on, but not for another five hours yet. Her fleece pyjamas helped against the biting cold, but she should be tucked up in bed where it was warm. She padded across the floor, her bare feet freezing, the thin carpet doing little to prevent the chill leaching up through the floorboards.

She entered the living room and drew to a halt. In the faint light from the hallway, she was able to make out the round blob of Merlin curled up and apparently sound asleep on the sofa, and in his bowl was a perfectly decent pile of cat biscuits, still uneaten from where she'd filled it up before bed.

Kerry exhaled a frustrated sigh. "Oh, you sod."

He'd clearly given up on the idea of food, but not after waking her first.

She wrapped her arms around her body and shivered again. It was freezing in here, more so than in the bedroom. Frowning, she stepped forward. The patio doors that led onto her ridiculously tiny balcony appeared not to be shut properly. How had they opened? It was the middle of winter, and she hadn't been out there recently. Even Merlin didn't want to go out when the air was freezing and more often than not, wet. There was no such thing as a white Christmas in London. A wet one, maybe, but that was all.

She'd gone back to her family home in Kent over the holiday period, though the few days she'd spent there had been awkward. She'd enjoyed meeting up with a couple of old school friends who had also not yet settled down with their own families and had made it back home for Christmas, but since her parents had split not long after she'd left for university—seven years ago now—it no longer really felt like home. It had been clear that her parents had only stayed together long enough for her to move out, probably waiting out the years, something she'd felt terrible about. But when her mother got a new boyfriend, things had turned tricky. Kerry didn't like Philip. He was younger than her mum and was the complete opposite to her dad. There was something about him that made her uncomfortable. She found he stared at her a little too long or got too far into her personal space when he spoke to her, so she'd made her excuses and gone to stay with her dad instead.

Kerry tore her thoughts away from her family and focused on the open doors. Moving closer, she craned her neck, trying to get a better view. Her stomach dropped, her breath catching. She should turn on the living room light, but she suddenly found herself in some kind of vortex that pulled her in towards the open doors and what she was seeing, and she couldn't break away.

The doors weren't just open. Beside the handle, on the side where the key had been sticking out of the lock, a circle had been cut in the glass, just big enough to fit a hand through.

Beyond that, the chicken wire she'd used to prevent the cat from launching himself off the balcony had also been cut and bent back.

No, she definitely hadn't left the doors open herself.

Someone else had opened them.

She suddenly became aware of another presence in the flat, of the prickling of hair standing on the back of her neck and the heavy weight of another person's gaze. Her breathing came fast—like it had when she'd first woken, short, sharp inhales through her nose. Her eyes pricked with tears of fright.

Her mind raced, trying to figure out what she should do next. What could possibly be the right action to take in this circumstance? If he'd come through the balcony doors, that meant the front door was still locked. The keys hung from a hook, together with her coat. There would be no way she'd be able to unhook the keys, and unlock the door, and escape without him catching her first.

Where had she left her phone? It was on charge beside the bed, she was sure. She didn't have a landline—there never seemed to be any point in paying two bills when she only ever used her mobile. Now she deeply regretted that. If there was a phone beside her, she might at least be able to grab it and punch in nine-nine-nine. Even if she didn't have time to speak, the dispatcher might have traced the call.

She had to run for the bedroom and somehow hope she got there before the intruder did.

Kerry dug her toes into the thin carpet, and a whine of fear escaped her throat. She sensed him standing there, hidden in the alcove that was her kitchen.

The flat was tiny—only made up of her bedroom, the bathroom, and the short hallway that led from the kitchen and living area to them both. If she could just get to the bedroom and slam the door behind her, maybe she would buy herself enough time to call for help? But how long would she really be able to hold him off? Maybe the bathroom would be better—at least there was a lock on the door. No, the phone was in the bedroom, and if she managed to lock herself in the bathroom, what would she do then? He was bound to get in eventually, and there were no windows in the bathroom for her to escape from. Could she hope the neighbours might hear the intruder trying to break down the door? Then she remembered how silently he'd let himself into her flat, how he'd cut glass and opened a door, with barely a sound, and she knew with solid certainty that he'd get into her bathroom just as easily and quickly.

No one would hear a thing.

She needed to make some noise. To scream as loudly as she could and pray someone would hear her and know something was wrong. But she also knew her moment of opportunity was short. He would silence her quickly enough.

In her head, she counted herself down. *Three... two... one.*

Kerry spun on her tiptoes and ran.

Never before had her flat seemed so long. Such a huge distance between the living room and the bedroom.

She found her voice. "Help! Somebody help me—"

A body slammed into her from behind, an arm winding around her middle, hauling her off her feet, the other around her face, large fingers clamping across her mouth.

On the sofa, Merlin shot out of his seat, fur erect as a ridge down his spine, tail puffed out, and vanished behind the furniture.

The hand over her mouth dulled her scream to a muffled mumble. He'd lifted her, so her bare feet cycled in the air. He was strong, and though she tried to thrash and wriggle in his grip, he carried her easily.

Where were they going? Into the bedroom?

A new kind of fear took over. He was going to rape her, and then there was a good chance he'd kill her. She didn't want to die. She was young and had such a bright future ahead of her. She hadn't had the chance to find the man she would marry or think about children. She'd never visited all those countries she'd promised herself she'd go to but never had, always too focused on getting her degree, and then finding the right job, in pushing ahead in her career as an accountant. How she wished she hadn't done that and had spent more time living instead of working. What about her parents? How would they cope without her? This was going to break her mum's heart.

She did her best to calm her racing thoughts and try to think. The bedroom! He was carrying her into the bedroom.

She'd wanted to come in here because this was also where her phone was. If she got her phone, she could call for help.

Still holding her from behind, one arm around her waist, the other clamped over her mouth, the intruder carried her over to the bed. She darted her gaze around, frantic, and it landed on the bedside table where her phone sat charging, screen facing up.

He threw her, facedown, on the bed, and she stretched her arm in the direction of the phone, desperate to grab it or snag the charging cord and use that to yank it towards her.

But his strong fingers wrapped around her throat from behind, fixing her attention back on him and her survival. She scrabbled at his hands, trying to yank them off, and then when it was proving impossible, she flailed backwards, hoping to strike him somewhere it would hurt. But she was facedown on the mattress, his weight pinning her, his hands around her throat. Her head was turned to the side, her cheek pressing into the pillow that had been nestling her head in sleep only a matter of minutes ago.

How had so much changed so fast?

Her gaze locked on the phone again, still plugged in, and Kerry stretched out her hand, reaching for the phone.

Her lungs burned, her windpipe down to the size of a straw, barely a whistle of air getting in and out. Her eyes bulged, and she imagined the colour of her face would be like an overripe piece of fruit. The muscles in her arms strained, her fingers clawed. Deep down, she knew it was over, but she couldn't bring herself to let go of that final thread of hope.

And as the last bubbles of oxygen dissolved from her blood, her eyes were still fixed on the phone.

Chapter Two

Lara Maher tugged on the front of the strapless black ballgown, certain it had slid down farther than it was supposed to. If it dropped any lower, she was going to flash her bra at all these posh people.

It was a charity auction for underprivileged children, all these wealthy, educated white people making themselves feel better by throwing money they wouldn't miss at people less fortunate.

Where the hell was Tristan?

She looked around for him anxiously. He'd promised he wouldn't leave her alone for too long, but this was business for him as well as pleasure. Not that it was pleasure for her. She'd been tempted to try to get out of coming, but she knew what his reaction would have been. He wanted her here—not only so he had someone on his arm, but also so he knew exactly what she was doing. He wouldn't have liked her to have an evening to herself. An evening of freedom. He would have questioned every single minute that she'd spent not in his presence, and, even then, she doubted he'd believe what she told him. Sometimes, she wondered why she bothered to speak at all, since he rarely seemed to believe what she said.

She caught the eye of a couple in their thirties, the woman with her arm looped through that of the man she was with, both in formal wear, as was required for the evening. The woman offered Lara a polite smile, and the man ducked his head in a nod. Heat flooded into her face at just that tiny amount of attention, and though Lara smiled back, she quickly glanced away so they didn't try to engage her in conversation. She never knew what to say to these people, completely out of her depth. If they asked her what she did, she'd tell them she ran her own business and hoped they left it at that. If she had to admit she was a cleaner, they'd turn their noses up at her. Oh, they might do a good job hiding their feelings, but those first few seconds were all Lara needed to see exactly what they thought of her.

"There you are."

She turned at Tristan's voice, her heart rate stepping up a notch. While she was relieved not to be standing alone anymore, she was often anxious in his presence.

He leaned in and kissed her cheek, his skin smooth and perfectly shaven. "You look beautiful, you know."

"Thanks. You scrub up pretty well yourself."

He beamed at her compliment. "The auctions are going to start any minute. Shall we go through?"

He offered his arm to her, and she took it, so they took the same stance as the couple who had smiled at her moments earlier.

"Here." He whisked a glass of champagne off a tray that someone carried around. "Just the one."

"I know." She raised a smile. "I wouldn't want any more than that."

Tristan had been in a surprisingly good mood these last couple of days, almost jovial, which wasn't like him at all, and she didn't want to say or do anything that would ruin his positive demeanour.

He placed his hand against her lower back and guided her towards the auction room. The majority of people already had their seats, and she experienced that flutter of panic that she wouldn't have anywhere to sit. It would show Tristan up, and he hated being shown up more than anything else.

"Mrs Maher," a man in a bow tie greeted them. "I'm so pleased you could make it."

She didn't correct him, sensing that men like him didn't like to have their mistakes pointed out.

"Thank you," she said, "it's been a wonderful evening."

"I'm glad you're having a nice time." Movement on stage, the crackle of a microphone jarring through the air. "Looks like we're about to get started. If you'll excuse me."

"Of course."

Tristan kissed her cheek. "I have to go and help. I'll be back when the auction is over. Make sure you don't bid on anything. Go and sit down."

He turned and walked away, and she shuffled along the row towards a couple of empty chairs, murmuring "Excuse me, sorry, excuse me" to the people she squeezed past.

She took a seat beside yet another well-dressed couple. They smiled at her politely, and she did her best to smile back, all the while praying they wouldn't try to engage her in conversation. If they asked her what she was bidding on, she'd have to be honest and tell them she knew nothing about art and was simply here as a guest.

The auction began, the booming voice of the auctioneer swelling into the magnificent space of the gallery. Lara was filled with the terrifying sense that she was going to accidentally bid some insane amount of money for something she didn't want. Around her, hands shot into the air, and figures—amounts that she made in a year—were called out.

How casually these people spent the sort of money that would change her life. Yes, she earned a wage, but it all went straight into the house, leaving nothing spare. Every single penny was accounted for, and if it wasn't, God help her. She kept every receipt, right down to a twenty-five pence envelope purchased down at her local post office. She swore the people who worked there thought she was just being difficult each time she asked them to print her out a receipt for every tiny thing she bought. Even when she smiled and explained it was for her bookkeeping, the slightly put-out expression never seemed to leave their faces.

Lara sat with her hands clamped between her thighs and her neck rigid, to prevent any crazy moments of unwanted bidding, and just wished for the whole thing to be done with.

At least out here, among all these people, I'm safe.

But she wasn't, not really. It was all a façade, this whole thing. All these beautifully put-together people, with their expensive clothes and professional hair and makeup, they were exactly like her underneath, flesh and bone. They were pretending to be kind and generous by bidding on items they probably didn't want in order to donate money to charity, but that wasn't what they were doing really. No, this was all a display, no different to the stags up in Richmond Park when the rutting season came along. These people were displaying their wealth, and wealth meant power.

She knew better than anyone, when you had nothing, you were helpless.

The auction came to an end, and she sagged in relief at the knowledge she'd got through it without doing anything crazy. Did she even trust herself anymore?

The weight of a hand pressed on her shoulder, and she jumped.

She'd been sitting there, staring into space, while everyone else had already left their seats and were most likely mingling back at the bar. Her own drink was still almost full, minus the single sip she'd taken.

"I'm almost done. Won't be too much longer, and then we can go home."

She smiled up at Tristan, trying to bring herself around. "Oh good. I am tired."

"Yes, you seem it. Is that why you're sitting here on your own? It's not making me look good. People will start asking questions."

She had no idea what sort of questions he was worried about—she doubted anyone had noticed her, the little mouse hiding in the corner—but that was Tristan through and through. He was so self-conscious, he always thought people were talking about him, judging him. Though he was successful and mingled with these kinds of people, a part of him always felt like he was the odd one out, like they were aware he wasn't really their type. That they saw through the veneer.

If only they knew.

Chapter Three

The naked body of a woman in her twenties was sitting up, her back against the padded headboard of the double bed. One knee was bent, the other straight out, and one hand rested on her flat stomach. Her blue eyes were open and staring, though the whites were both shot with blood, and her long blonde hair fell either side of her shoulders, the tips resting just above her breasts. Rigor mortis had set in. It was going to take a bit of work to get her into a body bag when the time came.

DI Erica Swift turned her face towards her shoulder slightly, trying to avoid the smell. Though the young woman was only thought to be dead a day or two, it was clearly enough for the decomposition process to have started.

Sergeant Diana Reynolds was in charge of the scene, and Erica was grateful for there to be another woman in the room. The strangely intimate way the body had been arranged made her feel as though the victim's privacy was being protected by there being more women with her than men. A SOCO officer was also present, and Reynolds pointed out places to leave numbers to designate what needed to be photographed and bagged up. Erica had already donned protective gloves and footwear before entering the scene—not just the bedroom, but the entire flat. It looked as though the intruder had broken in through the doors in the living room, and so would have walked the length of the flat to place the victim on the bed. Not a single part of the property would be left unturned.

"Kerry Norris," Reynolds said, introducing the victim, "twenty-seven years old and an accountant with Livingston Chartered Accountants in Waterloo East."

Erica stepped forwards, her gaze skirting over the body. "Any sign of sexual assault?"

"Nothing obvious, though we'll know more after the forensic pathology team have worked on her."

"She's been staged," Erica pointed out. "There's no way she died in that position."

Reynolds nodded. "Agreed. Someone definitely moved her after death."

Though Kerry Norris was naked, the position didn't appear overtly sexual. If anything, she seemed more relaxed, as though she might sit this way while watching television.

With a gloved hand, Erica gently lifted the blonde hair away from the victim's throat to reveal the dark bruises and red marks that hinted at a possible cause of death. They wouldn't know for sure until after the autopsy. Since the body was staged, it was possible the attacker had killed her in another way and then left the marks as a way to distract them. Over the years, she's learned never to assume, even if it looked obvious.

She let the hair drop back into place. "Any other apparent injuries?"

Reynolds pursed her lips. "Not that we've seen so far, though of course we haven't moved the body yet."

Voices signalled another arrival, and moments later, DS Shawn Turner entered the bedroom. They kept as few people in the room as possible. It was a small space, and Erica didn't want to risk too many feet trampling over evidence, and now there were four of them in here, including the SOCO officer and Reynolds.

His shirt was untucked, his jacket rumpled. He seemed frazzled, which was unlike him.

She eyed him up and down. "Where have you been?"

"Nowhere," he insisted.

"Yeah, right." She didn't believe him for a second.

His brown cheeks tinged with red.

"Hot date?" she guessed.

"I wasn't supposed to start my shift till later. I got interrupted."

She held up a hand. "I don't need to know what you got interrupted doing."

It was mid-morning—hardly the normal sort of time for a hook-up. Did that mean he had someone stay over then, or—judging by the state of his clothes—he'd stayed over there?

Shawn's personal life was definitely something he normally kept quiet about, and probably would have done on this occasion, too, had he not been called in about the body that had been discovered. She wasn't sure what it was, but there always seemed to be that little edge of discomfort about him whenever his personal life came up. Maybe it was simply that he preferred for one to not affect the other. She imagined that their DCI, Gibbs, probably liked that about Shawn.

Their violent crimes team had been expanded in its role to fill in wherever they were needed. Despite all their hard work, it was as though they were swimming upstream when it came to violence in the city. No matter how many people they arrested, how many youths they stopped and searched on the street, the occurrence of stabbings, and shootings, and domestic violence only increased. All the teams, including the murder squad, were overwhelmed with the number of cases that landed on their laps, and Erica went wherever she was needed. And, basically, wherever Gibbs told her to go. He was her boss, after all.

She quickly brought Shawn up to date with the case, and as she did so, a slender tabby cat meowed and curled itself around her legs.

"Get the cat out of here," she said. "It's going to make a mess of the crime scene."

Reynolds glanced down at the animal. "We've called the RSPCA. They're on their way. Hopefully, a family member will be able to take it in."

"Let's at least shut it in the bathroom until then. It's already walked all over the bed."

This wasn't a bloody crime scene, so at least there weren't little bloody paw prints all over everything, but she still didn't want the animal in the room with the body. Plenty of cats would have hidden away with this number of strangers around, but this one just seemed desperate for some attention. Her heart melted for a moment. Poor little thing. Poppy had been desperate for them to have a pet for ages now, but Erica couldn't give in to her daughter's demands, however guilty she felt about denying her something cute and furry to love. She had enough things she was trying to juggle without having to worry about a pet as well.

"Luckily, the cat had plenty of dried food and water down," Reynolds said, "or it could have been worse."

Erica grimaced. It was never much fun dealing with a crime scene when a beloved pet had been left without food or water and there was only one other source of food in the house.

Shawn bent and scooped up the cat and carried it into the bathroom and shut the door on it.

"I'd rather it wasn't in the building at all," she said, "but I'm not so heartless that I'd throw it out when it's clearly a house cat."

"Or at least, a flat cat," Shawn said, gesturing to their surroundings.

She smirked. "A flat cat? That sounds wrong."

He chuckled and then refocused on the body. "Who discovered the victim?"

"Her boss," Reynolds said. "She didn't turn up for work and so he tried calling. When she didn't show up the second day and still wasn't answering her phone, he came around to check on her. Seems the central heating comes on automatically, and with the bed so close to the radiator..."

She didn't need to say anything else, the smell of death in the room was an adequate explanation.

"So, he called us?" Erica prompted.

"Yes, he did."

"What's his name?"

"Mr Evan Ashworth. He's been taken down to the station, but I'm not sure how much help he's going to be. He didn't have a key for the flat, so the attending officers had to force entry, and he said he'd never been here before. He looked up her address in the human resources files."

"Let's see if we can get his prints anyway. If we find any in the flat, we'll know he's lying about never having been here."

She thought for a moment. "What about other friends or family? Or a boyfriend?" She looked around for photographs that would indicate Kerry Norris having had someone special in her life, but there were only a few framed photographs of who she assumed was the dead woman's mum and dad, and a couple of group photographs of her when she was younger, with her arms around a gaggle of girlfriends. "Have any been notified yet?"

"Not yet. I believe her family live in Kent."

Erica mentally calculated how long it would take for her to get there. She'd always prefer to break this kind of news in person, if at all possible. It was also a good opportunity to find out more about the victim and what kind of background she came from, though by the job Kerry Norris had done, and that she was able to afford a flat in London—even if it was East London—on her own, told her that she'd come from an affluent background and had benefitted from a good education.

"What about items missing from the flat?" Erica asked Reynolds. "Does anything appear to have been stolen—a burglary gone wrong?"

Reynolds gestured to the expensive iPhone sitting on the bedside table right next to the bed. "Whoever did this didn't take the phone, and there's a MacBook and a smart TV in the other room. Plus, her handbag is hung up on hooks near the front door and her purse is still inside it."

"Not a burglary then," Erica mused, "unless the person was looking for something specific—something that might be of value only to them.".

"We'll have to check with the family to see if anything like that is missing. The intruder got in through the living room doors that led out onto a small balcony. The balcony had chicken wire covering the front of it—I assume to prevent the cat from getting out—but a hole was cut in that as well."

Erica left the bedroom and walked through the flat to come to a halt at the balcony doors.

"We might get prints off the railings, though this all seems pretty slick. He's planned it, brought the right tools with him to make sure he got access to the property, so at the very least I expect he'd have worn gloves."

Shawn nodded. "Whoever broke in here came prepared. They knew what tools they'd need to get in."

She exhaled a long breath. "This was planned. Whoever did this knew exactly where they were going and what they were going to need to get in here."

Shawn cocked an eyebrow. "Possibly someone she knows, then? Someone who's been in here before?"

Erica let her gaze drift over the railings and the cut chicken wire.

"How did they get from the ground to the balcony?" she asked Reynolds.

Reynolds stepped forward and pointed to the left of the balcony. "There's a concrete canopy over the front door of the building. My guess is that they pulled over one of the black bins, climbed up onto that, then onto the canopy, and then onto the balcony."

"And then got out the same way?"

"The front door was locked and the keys still inside, so most likely, yes."

She needed to see it for herself. "Let's take a look outside."

The three of them left via the front door, removing protective outer wear as they went, aware they'd need to replace them with new ones when they went back into the flat.

Erica braced herself against the cold. Sometimes Januaries could be all crisp blue skies and mornings draped in pretty white frost, but this January had brought nothing but greyness and drizzle. It had been a difficult start to the year. Not only had they endured their first Christmas without Chris, but then she'd woken up on New Year's day and realised she'd have a whole other year to get through, and that it would just repeat for the rest of her life. She'd done her best to make the festive season as exciting as possible for Poppy, but she'd been acting the entire time. A part of her had been crushed in grief, and it had been almost impossible to push herself outwards from the grief instead of curling herself into a ball around it. They'd gone to Natasha's house for Christmas day, but it had been heart-breaking to wake up Christmas morning and for him not to be there. Poppy had woken up stupidly early as well, wanting to open her presents, and so by the time seven a.m. rolled around, there had been a long stretch of hours between then and going around to her sister's. As the months passed by without him, it sometimes seemed as though he'd been gone forever, but then other times his loss would hit her and she'd feel like it had only been days since his death.

The hurt never lessened, however, and neither did the anger. There were nights she spent lying awake, seething with fury, imagining all the things she'd say and do to Nicholas Bailey if she was ever to come face to face with him. She'd been having therapy sessions, which she'd cut back on, but perhaps it

ith thinning blond hair that revealed a pink scalp

ded them with cool grey eyes. "Yes? Can I help

ris?" she enquired, instinctively sensing this wasn't
ather.

loesn't live here anymore."

ntally kicked herself. She should have checked
nts were still together, rather than assuming.

out her ID. "I'm DI Swift, and this is DS Turner.
is around? We really need to speak to her. It's

narrowed a fraction, and then he turned to shout
ılder, "Caroline! There's some police here to see
ıked back to them. "She was just hanging the
"

till blocking the doorway.

ke to come in, Mr..." She trailed off, giving him
ı the gap.

ıe said. "Philip Reid."

d. This really is a sensitive matter. It's not a
we can have on the doorstep."

ed back again, as though to determine whether
line was coming and would tell him something
when she still didn't appear, he moved to one side
them in. They both stepped into the hallway, and
ront door behind them.

ıred to the room at the end of the hall. "Through

was time she started going again. She wanted to be able to trust in the system, and also trust herself that she would react in a way that was fitting to her position. She remembered how she'd felt when she'd caught the young man who'd been responsible for the murders at the East London University, how close she'd come to going too far.

Erica had checked up on Paige Arland a couple of times since October, and she was pleased that the young woman had remained on her course, despite what had happened. It took a lot of strength to confront everything and everyone when it would have been easier to run away.

The front of the building faced the road, and Erica stared up at it, her attention drawn to the black bars of the Juliette balcony and the chicken wire that now only half covered them. A tree partially hid the balcony from the properties across the street. In the summer, the view would have been obscured completely, but right now the branches were bare.

"Any chance of security cameras nearby?" she asked Reynolds. The street was purely residential, and they'd be lucky to get anything on camera.

"I've got a couple of officers going door-to-door, asking if anyone saw anything, or if any of them have home security cameras. We'll have to keep our fingers crossed on that one. We're assuming this happened during the night, but until we get an accurate time of death back from the autopsy, we won't know exactly when."

"What about others in the building? We need to find out if anyone saw or heard anything unusual. If there was shouting or banging, that might help us figure out the time this happened, as well. Also find out about the days leading up to her death.

Did anyone see her with someone, maybe she brought someone back? Find out if there was anyone hanging around during the days before her death. Someone must have sussed out the access to the flat, which means they got a good look at the place before they broke in."

Reynolds nodded. "Leave that with me. I'll make sure my officers cover everything."

"Great." Erica turned to Shawn. "Guess we'd better go and speak to the family."

There were few things wors[e] inform someone their love[d] worse when the people were the v

The news sat like a rock in She was about to destroy someo loved one killed was devastating murdered was earth-shattering. than anyone. She hated that she v pain in someone else, but it was to be done. Better that they hea media.

"You okay?" Shawn glanced

He was aware of everything there for her during those early fury and grief that she had barel understood that she knew what this family.

She sucked in a breath and done."

She swung open the car do house was a semi-detached, t bushes outside. Two mid-range

Erica rang the bell and step side.

The door swung open, and late thirties to early forties ap

and ra
beneat
He
you?"
"M
the vict
"N
Eric
that the
She
Is Mrs
importa
His
over his
you." H
washing
He w
"We'
space to f
"Reid
"Mr
conversat
He g
or not C
different,
and allow
he shut th
He ge
there."

A set of patio doors at the far end of the lounge opened out onto a small but tidy garden. The washing line was strung across the lawn, now bowed with clean, wet clothes neatly pinned to it. Approaching them from across the lawn, an empty plastic laundry basket tucked up under one arm, was a woman in her fifties. From the light, almost silvery-blonde hair, and the high cheekbones, and generous mouth, it was easy to tell this was Kerry Norris's mother.

Erica swallowed stomach acid as unaccustomed nerves at how she was about to shatter this poor woman's world churned inside her.

Caroline Norris caught sight of the two detectives standing in her lounge, and her attractive face crumpled with worry.

She entered through the patio doors and dropped the empty basket. "What's going on?"

"Mrs Norris, I'm DI Swift, and this is DS Turner."

"It's Ms Norris now. I kept my name, but I'm no longer married."

"Of course. Would you like to sit down?"

She glanced between them, her pale-blue eyes wide. "No, I wouldn't. Tell me what's going on. It's Kerry, isn't it? Has something happened to Kerry?"

"Please, take a seat."

"No, just tell me!"

"I'm sorry to tell you, but Kerry's body was discovered this morning. It would seem someone broke into her flat. We believe she was murdered."

"No." She shook her head. "Not Kerry. There must be some kind of mistake."

"There's no mistake. I'm sorry for your loss."

Her head continued to move in frantic little shakes. "It can't be Kerry."

"I'm so sorry, Ms Norris."

A wail of grief escaped her throat, and she fell to her knees. "No, Kerry! No, please, not my Kerry. Not my baby girl. Make it not be true."

Another scream of anguish pealed from her throat, and she rocked back and forth, her fingers knotted in her hair, her head bent.

Erica swallowed against a painful lump in her throat, her eyes pricking with tears of empathy at the other woman's grief.

"I'm so sorry," she said again, wishing she had something more.

Something better.

But no words would heal this kind of pain. Nothing would. People said time was a healer, but it wasn't. The wound was always as raw as that first day, you just got better at pretending you were fine.

She glanced over to where Philip Reid stood, his face pale, staring at the distressed woman on the floor, seemingly not knowing what to do. She noted how he didn't appear to be displaying any grief of his own, but she had no idea how well this man had known Kerry. She hoped he would at least offer some comfort to Kerry's mother.

"I understand this is a difficult time, but would it be possible to ask a few questions?" Erica didn't think she was going to get anything out of Caroline Norris but thought Reid might be able to tell them something. They would need to interview everyone in depth at some point, but now was not the time. She did, however, want to find out a couple of things

I thought the same. I got the impression things
easy in their homelife recently."

hat vibe, too. I'll do a background check on him, see
ything we should be concerned about."

rove to the address Reid had given them. This place
raced house—two-up, two-down—compressed
e adjacent buildings. She assumed Ms Norris must
family home in the divorce.

out a long breath, hating that she was going to have
vice in one day.

reak the news, if you want," Shawn offered.

w him a grateful smile but shook her head. "No, it's
it."

vas always the possibility he wouldn't be in, but
knocked—there was no bell—the door opened
tter of seconds.

clearly far older than the previous one, appeared in
y. Where Philip Reid was perhaps a decade younger
ne Norris, this man was most likely a decade older,
east twenty years between the two men. Was that
Norris hadn't liked her mother's new partner? Or
een more to it?

orris frowned between them. "Yes?"

nt through the routine of introducing themselves
o come in. "It's important," she added.

though you'll have to excuse the mess. I wasn't
isitors."

alked through into a compact living room, and he
r them to take a seat. The sofa had most likely been

about Caroline Norris's daughter, and she wanted to get a
better idea of who this man was in their home.

He nodded but bent to help Caroline up. She'd turned
into a ragdoll of a woman, her limbs hanging helplessly, her
legs appearing as though all the bones and muscles had been
removed. Philip half-carried her to the sofa. She continued
to howl, and he rubbed her back, but the gesture seemed
awkward.

"When was the last time you saw Kerry?" Erica asked.

"She was here for Christmas," Philip said. "Stayed a couple
of nights, but she went out with friends and hung out in her
room mostly."

"Did she seem okay? Any mention of confrontations she
might have had with anyone? Any problems?"

"I mean, she doesn't really tell me anything..." He trailed off
and glanced helplessly at Kerry's grieving mother.

She spoke in gasping little sobs. "No... one... would... want
to... hurt her. She was a good person!" She broke down again,
covering her face with her palms.

"And you're Ms Norris's boyfriend?" It felt strange to use
the term in relation to two clearly grown adults. "Partner?" she
added instead.

"That's right."

Erica threw a look towards Shawn and lifted her chin at
Philip. Shawn gave a slight nod to show he'd understood.

Philip Reid was staring around helplessly, as though
searching for a get out, and so Shawn gave him one. Just as
Erica had nodded at Shawn, Shawn now jerked his chin at
Philip to motion for the two of them to step away for a
moment.

Philip rose to his feet to join Shawn, and Erica slid into Philip's place, her hand placed on the other woman's back to try to offer her some comfort. Caroline's whole body shook and shuddered with the force of her grief.

Shawn stepped out of the room with Philip, enough to offer the illusion of privacy, while still being close enough for Erica to hear what was being said. Erica rubbed poor Caroline's back and strained her ears.

"How long have you been living here?" Shawn asked Philip.

The man's voice filtered through to her. "Almost twelve months now."

"How did Kerry feel about that?"

"I don't know." She could hear the shrug in his voice. "Like I said, she doesn't really tell me anything. I mean, *didn't* tell me anything."

"What about her father? Is he still around?"

"Yeah, he lives about twenty minutes away. She stayed with him, too, over the Christmas period, for longer than she spent here. I think Caroline was a bit hurt by it."

"Why did she stay longer with her father?" Shawn questioned.

"It's ridiculous really." He let out a long sigh. "They haven't been together for years, but she still didn't like the idea of her mother being in a new relationship."

"The two of you didn't get on then?"

"We never had the chance to get to know each other. We only met a handful of times."

Erica didn't think she was goi Kerry's poor mother right now, and hadn't broken the news to Mr Norris

"I'll be right back," she told Caro join Shawn and Philip.

"Would you like me to break th asked Reid.

Philip Reid nodded. "Yes, I thin haven't been talking lately. Things ar them."

"Do you have his current addres

Philip vanished into the kitchen that was addressed to Mr Steve N which had been crossed out and hi on the front.

He handed it to Erica. "Here forward this on, and never got roun

"Thank you. I'm sure we're goi but we'll leave you in peace, for the into the living room and raised he over the crying. "Mrs Norris, plea and know that we'll do everythi whoever did this to your daughter.'

Caroline Norris didn't appear said, but Philip Reid managed a no

Erica exchanged a tight smile v and left the house, pulling the fro She waited until they'd reached th

"What did you make of Philip

"Bit of a cold fish," Shawn said

purchased secondhand, and though he'd warned of a mess, the room, though tired, was tidy. They each took a seat.

Mr Norris looked between them. "Now, what's this all about?"

"I'm sorry to inform you that Kerry Norris's body was discovered at her flat this morning."

His eyes widened, and the colour fell from his face. "What?"

"Someone broke in. We believe she was murdered."

He clamped his hand over his mouth. "Murdered? Oh my God. Oh, poor Kerry. My poor girl."

His eyes grew glassy with unshed tears.

"We will need someone to come down and formally identify the body, but you don't have to do that right now. Take some time first."

He leaned forwards, his hands covering his mouth, his elbows between his knees.

"Who... who did this to her?"

"We plan on finding that out, Mr Norris. I truly am sorry for your loss. I understand this is difficult, but would you mind if I asked you a couple of questions? It might help us find out who was responsible for your daughter's death."

Numbly, he nodded.

"When did you last see or hear from Kerry?"

Erica was aware that Kerry's boss had noticed she was missing before her parents had. Were they not close?

"I'd sent her a couple of text messages a few days ago," he said, "but she hadn't answered. I'd just thought she was busy. She gets like that sometimes. I can go a week or more without hearing from her, and then it's like she's constantly on the phone or on a video chat. There doesn't seem to be any midpoint."

"Do you know if Kerry was seeing anyone?"

"No, I don't think so. No one she mentioned. No one serious, anyway."

"Any friends she might have fallen out with?"

He shook his head helplessly.

"What about any kinds of worrying behaviours? Drug or alcohol addictions?"

"No! Nothing like that. She works hard—" He broke off. "I mean, she worked hard." He clamped his hand to his mouth and choked back a sob. "Who did this? Who did this to my daughter?"

"That's what we're trying to find out, Mr Norris. Do you know of anyone who would have wanted to hurt or kill your daughter?"

"No, no one. She was a good girl. Everyone liked her."

"What was Kerry's relationship like with Philip Reid?"

He lifted his gaze, and his eyes flared with anger. "Do you think he might have done this to her? That son of a bitch."

She raised a calming hand. "No, please, that's not what we're saying at all. We need to cover all bases."

A whole body shudder went through him, and it was as though whatever strength he'd been holding on to rushed from him like the opening of a dam. He slumped into himself, crumpling, becoming physically smaller.

"Is there anyone we can call for you, Mr Norris?" Shawn asked. "Someone who can come and sit with you for a while?"

"No, I'd rather be on my own."

was time she started going again. She wanted to be able to trust in the system, and also trust herself that she would react in a way that was fitting to her position. She remembered how she'd felt when she'd caught the young man who'd been responsible for the murders at the East London University, how close she'd come to going too far.

Erica had checked up on Paige Arland a couple of times since October, and she was pleased that the young woman had remained on her course, despite what had happened. It took a lot of strength to confront everything and everyone when it would have been easier to run away.

The front of the building faced the road, and Erica stared up at it, her attention drawn to the black bars of the Juliette balcony and the chicken wire that now only half covered them. A tree partially hid the balcony from the properties across the street. In the summer, the view would have been obscured completely, but right now the branches were bare.

"Any chance of security cameras nearby?" she asked Reynolds. The street was purely residential, and they'd be lucky to get anything on camera.

"I've got a couple of officers going door-to-door, asking if anyone saw anything, or if any of them have home security cameras. We'll have to keep our fingers crossed on that one. We're assuming this happened during the night, but until we get an accurate time of death back from the autopsy, we won't know exactly when."

"What about others in the building? We need to find out if anyone saw or heard anything unusual. If there was shouting or banging, that might help us figure out the time this happened, as well. Also find out about the days leading up to her death.

Did anyone see her with someone, maybe she brought someone back? Find out if there was anyone hanging around during the days before her death. Someone must have sussed out the access to the flat, which means they got a good look at the place before they broke in."

Reynolds nodded. "Leave that with me. I'll make sure my officers cover everything."

"Great." Erica turned to Shawn. "Guess we'd better go and speak to the family."

Chapter Four

There were few things worse in this job than having to inform someone their loved one was dead. It was even worse when the people were the victim's parents.

The news sat like a rock in the middle of Erica's chest. She was about to destroy someone's world forever. Having a loved one killed was devastating enough, but for them to be murdered was earth-shattering. Erica knew that now better than anyone. She hated that she was about to instil that kind of pain in someone else, but it was part of her job, and it needed to be done. Better that they hear it from her than from social media.

"You okay?" Shawn glanced over in concern.

He was aware of everything she'd been through, had been there for her during those early days when she was so full of fury and grief that she had barely known how to function. He understood that she knew what this news was going to do to this family.

She sucked in a breath and nodded. "Yeah, let's just get it done."

She swung open the car door and climbed out. The Norris house was a semi-detached, tidy property with manicured bushes outside. Two mid-range vehicles sat in the driveway.

Erica rang the bell and stepped back slightly, Shawn by her side.

The door swung open, and a man she guessed to be in his late thirties to early forties appeared in the gap. He was tall and rangy, with thinning blond hair that revealed a pink scalp beneath.

He regarded them with cool grey eyes. "Yes? Can I help you?"

"Mr Norris?" she enquired, instinctively sensing this wasn't the victim's father.

"No, he doesn't live here anymore."

Erica mentally kicked herself. She should have checked that the parents were still together, rather than assuming.

She took out her ID. "I'm DI Swift, and this is DS Turner. Is Mrs Norris around? We really need to speak to her. It's important."

His eyes narrowed a fraction, and then he turned to shout over his shoulder, "Caroline! There's some police here to see you." He looked back to them. "She was just hanging the washing out."

He was still blocking the doorway.

"We'd like to come in, Mr..." She trailed off, giving him space to fill in the gap.

"Reid," he said. "Philip Reid."

"Mr Reid. This really is a sensitive matter. It's not a conversation we can have on the doorstep."

He glanced back again, as though to determine whether or not Caroline was coming and would tell him something different, but when she still didn't appear, he moved to one side and allowed them in. They both stepped into the hallway, and he shut the front door behind them.

He gestured to the room at the end of the hall. "Through there."

A set of patio doors at the far end of the lounge opened out onto a small but tidy garden. The washing line was strung across the lawn, now bowed with clean, wet clothes neatly pinned to it. Approaching them from across the lawn, an empty plastic laundry basket tucked up under one arm, was a woman in her fifties. From the light, almost silvery-blonde hair, and the high cheekbones, and generous mouth, it was easy to tell this was Kerry Norris's mother.

Erica swallowed stomach acid as unaccustomed nerves at how she was about to shatter this poor woman's world churned inside her.

Caroline Norris caught sight of the two detectives standing in her lounge, and her attractive face crumpled with worry.

She entered through the patio doors and dropped the empty basket. "What's going on?"

"Mrs Norris, I'm DI Swift, and this is DS Turner."

"It's Ms Norris now. I kept my name, but I'm no longer married."

"Of course. Would you like to sit down?"

She glanced between them, her pale-blue eyes wide. "No, I wouldn't. Tell me what's going on. It's Kerry, isn't it? Has something happened to Kerry?"

"Please, take a seat."

"No, just tell me!"

"I'm sorry to tell you, but Kerry's body was discovered this morning. It would seem someone broke into her flat. We believe she was murdered."

"No." She shook her head. "Not Kerry. There must be some kind of mistake."

"There's no mistake. I'm sorry for your loss."

Her head continued to move in frantic little shakes. "It can't be Kerry."

"I'm so sorry, Ms Norris."

A wail of grief escaped her throat, and she fell to her knees. "No, Kerry! No, please, not my Kerry. Not my baby girl. Make it not be true."

Another scream of anguish pealed from her throat, and she rocked back and forth, her fingers knotted in her hair, her head bent.

Erica swallowed against a painful lump in her throat, her eyes pricking with tears of empathy at the other woman's grief.

"I'm so sorry," she said again, wishing she had something more.

Something better.

But no words would heal this kind of pain. Nothing would. People said time was a healer, but it wasn't. The wound was always as raw as that first day, you just got better at pretending you were fine.

She glanced over to where Philip Reid stood, his face pale, staring at the distressed woman on the floor, seemingly not knowing what to do. She noted how he didn't appear to be displaying any grief of his own, but she had no idea how well this man had known Kerry. She hoped he would at least offer some comfort to Kerry's mother.

"I understand this is a difficult time, but would it be possible to ask a few questions?" Erica didn't think she was going to get anything out of Caroline Norris but thought Reid might be able to tell them something. They would need to interview everyone in depth at some point, but now was not the time. She did, however, want to find out a couple of things about Caroline Norris's daughter, and she wanted to get a better idea of who this man was in their home.

He nodded but bent to help Caroline up. She'd turned into a ragdoll of a woman, her limbs hanging helplessly, her legs appearing as though all the bones and muscles had been removed. Philip half-carried her to the sofa. She continued to howl, and he rubbed her back, but the gesture seemed awkward.

"When was the last time you saw Kerry?" Erica asked.

"She was here for Christmas," Philip said. "Stayed a couple of nights, but she went out with friends and hung out in her room mostly."

"Did she seem okay? Any mention of confrontations she might have had with anyone? Any problems?"

"I mean, she doesn't really tell me anything..." He trailed off and glanced helplessly at Kerry's grieving mother.

She spoke in gasping little sobs. "No... one... would... want to... hurt her. She was a good person!" She broke down again, covering her face with her palms.

"And you're Ms Norris's boyfriend?" It felt strange to use the term in relation to two clearly grown adults. "Partner?" she added instead.

"That's right."

Erica threw a look towards Shawn and lifted her chin at Philip. Shawn gave a slight nod to show he'd understood.

Philip Reid was staring around helplessly, as though searching for a get out, and so Shawn gave him one. Just as Erica had nodded at Shawn, Shawn now jerked his chin at Philip to motion for the two of them to step away for a moment.

Philip rose to his feet to join Shawn, and Erica slid into Philip's place, her hand placed on the other woman's back to try to offer her some comfort. Caroline's whole body shook and shuddered with the force of her grief.

Shawn stepped out of the room with Philip, enough to offer the illusion of privacy, while still being close enough for Erica to hear what was being said. Erica rubbed poor Caroline's back and strained her ears.

"How long have you been living here?" Shawn asked Philip.

The man's voice filtered through to her. "Almost twelve months now."

"How did Kerry feel about that?"

"I don't know." She could hear the shrug in his voice. "Like I said, she doesn't really tell me anything. I mean, *didn't* tell me anything."

"What about her father? Is he still around?"

"Yeah, he lives about twenty minutes away. She stayed with him, too, over the Christmas period, for longer than she spent here. I think Caroline was a bit hurt by it."

"Why did she stay longer with her father?" Shawn questioned.

"It's ridiculous really." He let out a long sigh. "They haven't been together for years, but she still didn't like the idea of her mother being in a new relationship."

"The two of you didn't get on then?"

"We never had the chance to get to know each other. We only met a handful of times."

Erica didn't think she was going to get anything from Kerry's poor mother right now, and she was aware they still hadn't broken the news to Mr Norris.

"I'll be right back," she told Caroline, and got to her feet to join Shawn and Philip.

"Would you like me to break the news to her father?" she asked Reid.

Philip Reid nodded. "Yes, I think that would be best. They haven't been talking lately. Things are a little fractious between them."

"Do you have his current address?"

Philip vanished into the kitchen and returned with a letter that was addressed to Mr Steve Norris at this address, but which had been crossed out and his new address handwritten on the front.

He handed it to Erica. "Here you go. I kept meaning to forward this on, and never got round to it."

"Thank you. I'm sure we're going to have other questions, but we'll leave you in peace, for the moment." She stepped back into the living room and raised her voice slightly to be heard over the crying. "Mrs Norris, please, accept our condolences and know that we'll do everything in our power to catch whoever did this to your daughter."

Caroline Norris didn't appear to register what had been said, but Philip Reid managed a nod.

Erica exchanged a tight smile with Shawn, and they turned and left the house, pulling the front door shut behind them. She waited until they'd reached their car before she spoke.

"What did you make of Philip Reid?"

"Bit of a cold fish," Shawn said.

"Yeah, I thought the same. I got the impression things haven't been easy in their homelife recently."

"I got that vibe, too. I'll do a background check on him, see if there's anything we should be concerned about."

Erica drove to the address Reid had given them. This place was a terraced house—two-up, two-down—compressed between the adjacent buildings. She assumed Ms Norris must have got the family home in the divorce.

She let out a long breath, hating that she was going to have to do this twice in one day.

"I can break the news, if you want," Shawn offered.

She threw him a grateful smile but shook her head. "No, it's fine. I'll do it."

There was always the possibility he wouldn't be in, but when Erica knocked—there was no bell—the door opened within a matter of seconds.

A man, clearly far older than the previous one, appeared in the doorway. Where Philip Reid was perhaps a decade younger than Caroline Norris, this man was most likely a decade older, putting at least twenty years between the two men. Was that why Kerry Norris hadn't liked her mother's new partner? Or had there been more to it?

Steve Norris frowned between them. "Yes?"

She went through the routine of introducing themselves and asked to come in. "It's important," she added.

"Okay, though you'll have to excuse the mess. I wasn't expecting visitors."

They walked through into a compact living room, and he gestured for them to take a seat. The sofa had most likely been purchased secondhand, and though he'd warned of a mess, the room, though tired, was tidy. They each took a seat.

Mr Norris looked between them. "Now, what's this all about?"

"I'm sorry to inform you that Kerry Norris's body was discovered at her flat this morning."

His eyes widened, and the colour fell from his face. "What?"

"Someone broke in. We believe she was murdered."

He clamped his hand over his mouth. "Murdered? Oh my God. Oh, poor Kerry. My poor girl."

His eyes grew glassy with unshed tears.

"We will need someone to come down and formally identify the body, but you don't have to do that right now. Take some time first."

He leaned forwards, his hands covering his mouth, his elbows between his knees.

"Who... who did this to her?"

"We plan on finding that out, Mr Norris. I truly am sorry for your loss. I understand this is difficult, but would you mind if I asked you a couple of questions? It might help us find out who was responsible for your daughter's death."

Numbly, he nodded.

"When did you last see or hear from Kerry?"

Erica was aware that Kerry's boss had noticed she was missing before her parents had. Were they not close?

"I'd sent her a couple of text messages a few days ago," he said, "but she hadn't answered. I'd just thought she was busy. She gets like that sometimes. I can go a week or more without hearing from her, and then it's like she's constantly on the phone or on a video chat. There doesn't seem to be any midpoint."

"Do you know if Kerry was seeing anyone?"

"No, I don't think so. No one she mentioned. No one serious, anyway."

"Any friends she might have fallen out with?"

He shook his head helplessly.

"What about any kinds of worrying behaviours? Drug or alcohol addictions?"

"No! Nothing like that. She works hard—" He broke off. "I mean, she worked hard." He clamped his hand to his mouth and choked back a sob. "Who did this? Who did this to my daughter?"

"That's what we're trying to find out, Mr Norris. Do you know of anyone who would have wanted to hurt or kill your daughter?"

"No, no one. She was a good girl. Everyone liked her."

"What was Kerry's relationship like with Philip Reid?"

He lifted his gaze, and his eyes flared with anger. "Do you think he might have done this to her? That son of a bitch."

She raised a calming hand. "No, please, that's not what we're saying at all. We need to cover all bases."

A whole body shudder went through him, and it was as though whatever strength he'd been holding on to rushed from him like the opening of a dam. He slumped into himself, crumpling, becoming physically smaller.

"Is there anyone we can call for you, Mr Norris?" Shawn asked. "Someone who can come and sit with you for a while?"

"No, I'd rather be on my own."

Erica slid a card across the coffee table. "If you think of anything, please call me. Any time, day or night."

He nodded but didn't pick up the card.

Erica exchanged a glance with Shawn, who gave a slight tilt of his head to say it was time to go. They still wanted to speak with Kerry's boss, who had been the one to alert them to the crime.

"We're sorry for your loss," she said again, rising to her feet.

He fixed her with tear-filled eyes. "Just find out who did this. Make the bastard pay. Because if you don't, I will."

"We're doing everything we can."

Chapter Five

Within an hour and a half, they were back at the station and sitting opposite Kerry Norris's boss.

Evan Ashworth could have passed for one of their detectives, if it were not for the fact he was sitting on the wrong side of the table in one of their interview rooms. He was in his fifties, dressed in an expensive suit, and wore a constantly concerned expression, his brows pulled together, his forehead furrowed. He nursed a cup of vending machine coffee, which Shawn had got for him after they'd first arrived and had introduced themselves, then sat down to ask him some questions.

"Could you please state your full name?" Erica asked him.

"Mr Evan Quinton Ashworth," he replied.

"And your date of birth?"

"Seventeen of February, Nineteen Seventy."

"And your current address?"

He reeled it off.

Erica glanced down at her notes to check the place of work. "How long have you been working at Livingston Chartered Accountants?"

He frowned as he thought for a moment. "Fifteen years now."

"And how long have you known Kerry Norris?"

He exhaled a breath. "Only a couple of years. Just since she started at the accountants."

Erica jotted it down and then looked back up. "Now, talk me through exactly what happened before you found her. Start from when you woke up."

He shrugged. "It was just a normal morning. I got up, showered, dressed, drove to work. Kerry hadn't shown up the previous day, and when I asked after her, no one had heard from her. She's normally in the office by eight, as are most of us who work there, and by the time it was approaching nine, I figured she wasn't going to show up again. I had a meeting not far from where she lived, so I thought I'd stop by and just check up on her."

"And what time would you say you arrived at her flat?"

He checked his watch, as though that would give him the answer. "My meeting was at ten, so it was before then. I guess nine-thirtyish. I rang the bell downstairs but didn't get an answer, so I tried the communal front door, and it opened. I guess one of the other residents left it unlocked. Then I walked up the stairs to the front door of her flat, and knocked there, but didn't get any answer again. I went to call through the keyhole, and that's when I caught the smell." He pulled a face at the memory.

The central heating had come on by then, clearly set on a timer, and it had been a couple of days since the victim's murder, though they still hadn't had the exact time of death back yet.

"And that's when you called nine-nine-nine?"

He nodded. "That's right. I waited until a couple of uniformed officers arrived and then told them what I knew. They gained access to the property, and that was when they found her." He closed his eyes briefly, as though trying to block the thought of Kerry's dead, naked body from his mind. "It was obvious she was dead from their reaction, and then I was asked to come here and wait, which I did." His lips thinned. "I had to cancel my meeting, but obviously the client understood."

Erica didn't really care about their client when a young woman was dead.

"When was the last time Kerry Norris came into work?" Erica asked him.

The furrows in his forehead deepened. "It was three days ago now."

"So, she missed two days of work, including today."

"That's right."

"Do you often make house calls to your staff when one of them doesn't show up for work?"

"No, because I can normally get hold of them, or at least a family member, if they're really ill and can't get to the phone. It was extremely out of character not only for her to not have contacted the office to say why she wouldn't be in, but also to have her phone off."

"How would you describe Kerry?" she asked.

"Young, intelligent, outgoing, sociable. Everything you could ask for from a junior accountant. She was a pleasure to have around."

"Did she ever talk about people she might be involved with—a boyfriend, perhaps?"

"No, not at all. I got the impression she was content with focusing on her career, but then those weren't really the sort of conversations I'd have with any of my younger staff members. You'd be better asking some of her colleagues who were closer to her."

"Can we get their names?"

"Yes, of course. I'll write them down for you."

Erica pushed a piece of paper and a pen over to him, and he jotted down several names before pushing it back again.

"Thank you." She folded her hands together on the table. "Mr Ashworth, do you know of anyone who might have wanted to kill or hurt Kerry Norris?"

He shook his head. "No, sorry. I don't."

Erica went back over some of the points he'd mentioned, but there really didn't seem to be anything more he could tell them. Perhaps the victim's other colleagues could give them more of an insight into Kerry Norris's life.

"Thank you for your time, Mr Ashworth. If there's anything else you think of, please, let me know."

She handed him a business card.

"I really hope you find who did this. Kerry really was a lovely young woman. She'll be missed."

"We'll do everything we can," she said, rising to show him out of the station.

Chapter Six

Lara Maher juggled her mop and bucket, and bag of cleaning products, and used her key to open the front door of the house she was due to clean.

Normally, her elderly client was out at this time—doing a trip to the supermarket or perhaps taking a class down at the local hall—but the moment she stepped inside, Lara knew she wasn't alone. Muffled sobs came from the direction of the living room, and they didn't abate when Lara closed the front door again, deliberately louder, to announce her arrival.

"Hello?" she called out hesitantly. "Mrs Winthorpe?"

No answer came, and she crossed the entrance hall to the living room door. It was open a crack, and she reached out and lightly touched it. The door swung open easily, but still she didn't enter. Should she have knocked? She was out of her depth in this situation, like she was going to do something wrong, but she couldn't just turn away. The old lady was clearly distressed.

Lara sucked in a breath then stepped through into the room, taking in the chintzy, over-stuffed furniture, a mantelpiece filled with knick-knacks that Lara painstakingly dusted every other week, when she came. The house always had that slightly musty smell, no matter how many windows she opened or how much furniture polish she used.

"Mrs Winthorpe," she said again. "Is everything okay?"

She felt stupid asking the question, when evidently everything *wasn't* okay, but she didn't know what else to say.

The old lady was sitting in the high-back chair in the window, a bundled-up wad of tissues pressed to her face. She barely seemed to notice that Lara had arrived, so Lara crossed the room and crouched beside her. She reached out and touched the back of the woman's crepe-paper hand.

"What's happened? What's wrong?"

Lara glanced to the coffee table. Several bills with red headers lay strewn across the surface.

Mrs Winthorpe finally lowered the tissues from her eyes. "I'm so sorry, Lara, love, but I'm going to have to let you go."

Lara's heart dropped. Tristan wasn't going to be happy about her losing a job, but she would have to do her best to convince him that she could make up her hours somewhere else. She charged Mrs Winthorpe her lowest rate, anyway, and only came here every other week. It wasn't really much money, but to Tristan, every penny counted.

"You know I've loved having you come here," the old lady continued. "It makes everything else easier, with my legs being the way they are, but I can't afford to keep paying you."

She had swollen legs—oedema, Lara thought it was called—and struggled to get around. She was able to do the day-to-day stuff, such as wiping down the kitchen surfaces, but getting down to clean a bath or toilet was beyond her.

Lara patted her hand. "That's okay, Mrs Winthorpe, don't worry."

"I do, dear. I do. I'm not sure how I'm going to cope, and I feel so bad letting you down as well, but I simply can't afford to keep you on."

Lara hesitated, unsure what to do. Though she worried about herself, she also didn't want to leave the poor lady unable to manage the house.

"Isn't there some kind of help you can get from the social?" she asked. "A carer or someone who can come around?"

She sniffed and shook her head. "I've looked into it, but apparently I'm still too mobile."

"What about your sons? Can't they do something to help?"

Mrs Winthorpe always seemed to be alone. She had grown children, two sons, but one living in Canada with his own family now, and the other seemed to be a waste of space. He was in his forties, but never held down a job or had a permanent place to live.

"They don't have any money." She sighed, a shuddering sound. "And I hate to ask. A mother should be looking after her children, not the other way around."

"They're hardly children now, are they?"

"When you're a mother, dear, you'll understand. No matter how old they get, they're always your children."

Lara didn't have any, and she hoped it would stay that way. The thought of bringing innocent lives into her situation filled her with horror. Life was hard enough as it was, without having to worry about a helpless infant.

"And I'm sure they care about you and would want to help if you're struggling."

"You're a good girl. I bet your mother feels lucky to have you."

The mention of her own mother struck her with a winding pain, like a punch to the chest. "Oh, she died when I was a teenager."

Mrs Winthorpe's eyes filled with sympathy. "I'm so sorry to hear that."

"Thank you." Lara couldn't just abandon the old lady. "Look, how about I still clean for you? I'm here now, and I hate to see you struggling."

"I can't ask you to do that. You'd be working for nothing."

The bills on the table caught her attention. "What about those? Can you pay them?"

"I don't think so. I'm going to have to get in touch with both the telephone company and the power to beg them not to cut me off."

Lara glanced at the bills again. They weren't for large amounts—the telephone was twenty-nine pounds, and the gas and electric were even less. One woman living alone didn't use much.

She suddenly became aware of the paper envelope of folded notes in her back pocket. Her previous client had paid in cash, and paid her once a month, so it added up. It was enough to cover Mrs Winthorpe's overdue bills.

What's Tristan going to say when I don't come home with the money?

She could make something up. She'd say that she lost it, or that the client hadn't been able to get to the bank. There was no way she'd tell him the truth—he wouldn't be happy about that at all. She knew exactly what he'd say: she cared more about other people than she did him. It was always a competition with Tristan when it came to her. Any attention she dared give anything other than him always went down badly.

There was a post office right down the road. It would only take her a minute, and so much worry would be lifted from

Mrs Winthorpe's shoulders. True, that worry would then be transferred to hers, but it would be worth it if only to stop the poor lady from crying. Lara didn't think she could walk out of here—after she'd cleaned or not—leaving her in tears.

She picked up the final notice bills from the table. "Is this all of them?"

"Yes, it is."

"I'll be back in ten minutes. Let's get these paid off for you."

Mrs Winthorpe reached for her. "Oh, no. I can't possibly expect you to do that."

"I want to. Really. It'll only take me ten minutes, and then you won't have to worry about them."

"You can't possibly afford to do that. I mean," she waved a hand around her home, "you're a cleaner."

Lara forced a smile. "I clean because I like to clean," she lied, "not because I need the money."

Now she felt bad for taking money from Mrs Winthorpe all the previous weeks when she'd clearly been struggling. Did it make her look bad for accepting it when she was now claiming that she scrubbed other people's toilets for a jolly?

"I'll be back shortly to do your clean. Don't worry about it."

She rose to her feet, still clutching the bills, and hurried back the way she'd come letting herself out of the front door with Mrs Winthorpe's protests echoing after her.

Lara was terrified Tristan would see her and demand to know what she was doing. Her fear was irrational, wasn't it? Tristan would be at work. But then it wouldn't be the first time he'd followed her during the day. His flexibility in his job meant he was able to sneak out. He kept her rota in his phone, so he knew exactly which jobs she was working and where she'd be and at what time. Sometimes, she'd spot his car pulling away from the kerb as she left a house, carrying all her mops and buckets with her. She'd catch his eye, so he'd be aware she'd seen him, but neither of them ever mentioned it when she got home or when she went to meet him from his work. He *wanted* her to know he kept a watchful eye on her, just to make sure she never tried to get one over on him.

At the post office, she joined the queue of customers and waited her turn. Her heart felt like it was in her throat, as though she was doing something terrible instead of trying to do an old lady a favour. She glanced over her shoulder, certain she'd spot Tristan lurking in the doorway, but only caught the eye of the young mother waiting in line behind her.

I don't have to do this. I could just turn around and walk out.

But she couldn't imagine the disappointment in Mrs Winthorpe's eyes if she went back with the bills unpaid. How could she explain that?

I'm sorry, Mrs Winthorpe, but I'm afraid of what the repercussions might be.

Then she would have to explain her situation and she'd rather take a whole week's worth of abuse than do that. She was so ashamed. She knew what people would say—that she should just leave—but it wasn't that easy. She had nothing. No money, no friends, no place of her own. She'd have to live on the street, and even if she did that, he would find her.

She reached the front of the line and approached the counter. This was her final chance to back out, but she was going to go through with it. She pushed the bills towards the middle-aged woman sitting behind the counter, and then took out the money and counted out the cash to pay them off. She was left with ten pounds remaining and she swallowed hard.

Tristan was going to be furious.

The woman accepted the money and gave her receipts for the payments. Lara thanked her and took them, clutching them tight in her fist. She was preparing herself to be accosted on the street, for him to demand to know what she was doing. She'd have no choice but to tell him the truth, in that case. But as she left the post office and turned back in the direction of Mrs Winthorpe's house, nothing happened. She didn't see Tristan's car.

She picked up her pace and hurried back. She let herself back in to the sound of the kettle boiling. She discovered the old lady in the kitchen, busying herself with a couple of mugs.

"I thought the least I could do to say thank you was make you a cup of tea."

"There's really no need, Mrs Winthorpe."

"Oh, nonsense." She flapped her away. "It's the least I could do. I might have a packet of biscuits around here somewhere."

"I'll get started while you find them," Lara said.

A warmth had blossomed in her chest at the sight of the old lady bustling around the kitchen, her tears now dried. But ice crept in around the edges of the warmth, shrinking it smaller and smaller, like a lake freezing in winter, until eventually, all that was left was the chill.

Chapter Seven

Erica had worked late on the case, then picked Poppy up from her sister's house when she'd finished, aware she wasn't going to get to spend any quality time with her daughter before she'd have to head back into the office the following morning.

She doubted there would ever be a time where she didn't feel the tug between her family and her work. She was lucky to have Natasha's support, and their father, Frank, was settled at Willow Glade Care Home now. That side of things, at least, had grown easier to cope with.

The next morning, after she'd dropped Poppy off at the school's breakfast club, she received a text from Shawn telling her to meet him at the borough's mortuary office. The pathologist had already worked on Kerry Norris and had a report for them, and Shawn knew she preferred to get the report direct. She hoped it would give them some clues, or at least point them in the right direction as to who was responsible for the young woman's death. She hoped for the same from the report from SOCO, which should come in at some point that day. She'd sent DC Rudd and Howard to speak with Kerry's colleagues, but none of them could tell them about someone who might have wanted to see Kerry hurt. They'd all had the same impression of her—hardworking, committed to her job, dated casually, but hadn't met anyone she'd mentioned lately.

Erica's thoughts went back to the mother's boyfriend, Philip Reid. Currently, their relationship seemed to be the only point of friction in Kerry Norris's life, but though Erica hadn't warmed to the man, that didn't mean he was capable of murdering his girlfriend's daughter. She wanted to find out what he was doing the night of Kerry's death, however, just to rule him out.

She pulled into the carpark of the mortuary office and spotted Shawn's car already there. He must have seen her in his rear-view mirror, as the driver's door opened and he climbed out. She swung the car into the empty space next to him, killed the engine, and got out as well.

"Sleep well?" She teased him about his night before. "No one keep you up all night?"

He didn't rise to it. "I slept fine. You?"

She rolled her eyes. "When do I ever sleep?"

Sometimes she thought she'd programmed herself to only manage on four or five hours a night. Anything more was a luxury.

Side by side, they entered the building and gave the receptionist their reason for being there.

She picked up the phone. "I'll give Dr Hamilton a call and let him know you're here."

"Oh, it's Dr Hamilton today?"

Erica tried to hide her disappointment that they wouldn't be working with Lucy Kim. She preferred Kim to Dr John Hamilton, who was an older man with near-white hair that was receding at the top but had been grown long at the back, creating a kind of mullet. He was a serious man, one of those people who, if you got seated beside him at a dinner party, you might find your heart sinking a little. Unless you had a particular appetite for discussing autopsies over a meal, of course.

"Kim's on holiday," the receptionist said. "Gone to Singapore to visit some family, I believe."

"Lucky her. Must be nice to see some blue sky."

London seemed to have been cast in a perpetual gloom for weeks now. On the run-up to Christmas, they'd had nothing but rain—with zero chance of that magical but utterly elusive white Christmas—and the clouds hadn't lifted into the new year either. Erica didn't mind the winter when it was all crisp, clear mornings, and frost on the ground, even if she did hate getting up in the dark and coming home in the dark, no matter what shift she worked, but this constant grey was just depressing. She envied Lucy Kim her holiday. Maybe that's what she should do once this case was over? She could book some time off and take Poppy away somewhere. It didn't need to be far, so they didn't have a long plane ride, but somewhere in the sunshine where Poppy could play on a beach or in a pool, and they could eat ice cream guilt-free.

The trouble was that nothing came guilt-free anymore. While she still needed to raise Poppy to have as normal a life as possible, nothing felt normal. Even the thought of going away, just the two of them, filled her with sorrow. There was always this missing spot between them, the person who should be filling the empty seat on the plane, or who she should be sitting on the balcony with late in the evening when Poppy was asleep, sharing a bottle of wine and enjoying the view.

She realised Shawn had said something. "What, sorry?"

"I said that we could do with a lead on this one. So far, we have no suspects and no witnesses. If the body can tell us something, we could use all the help we can get."

Erica nodded. "Yes, you're right. I don't want to have to go back to those poor parents and tell them that we have absolutely no idea who did this to their daughter. They deserve better than that."

The receptionist put down the phone. "You can go down to him now. He's expecting you."

Erica thanked the other woman, and they pushed through the doors that led to the stairwell, taking them down to the basement lab where Dr Hamilton waited for them.

"Thanks for coming down so fast," he said, shaking both their hands. "I wish I could give you something more solid to go on so you can find the suspect, but whoever did this has been meticulous about not leaving any DNA behind."

Erica's heart sank. That wasn't the news she'd wanted to hear.

They donned protective clothing and entered the examination room. The shape of a body lay beneath a sheet on the surgical table, and Dr Hamilton went to it and pulled back the sheet, revealing the body of the young woman beneath.

"Cause of death was acute cerebral anoxia via strangulation." He gestured to the neck. "The marks around the throat and compression and occlusion of the trachea indicate a manual strangulation rather than ligature or hanging."

"You mean he used his hands," she double-checked.

"That's right. I found blood in the oropharynx, and she suffered conjunctival petechial haemorrhage, which are the tiny red dots around the whites of the eyes, both a result of the strangulation. I'd estimate her time of death to be some time between seventy-two and sixty-five hours ago. The victim had a slightly elevated blood alcohol level, but not so high that it would have affected her reactions. No prescription drugs were found in her system. She was also on a birth control implant which I located in the inside of her upper arm."

Shawn glanced over at Erica. "That suggests she either had a relationship or was having regular enough sex to consider herself needing a contraceptive."

She shrugged. "Or she might have been on it for other reasons? She may have been on birth control to regulate periods."

Taking control of her fertility didn't necessarily mean Kerry Norris was having regular sex. She might have just been having it often enough that she didn't want there to be any accidents. She was a career woman and clearly didn't picture children in her near future."

"I also found a number of cat hairs on the body," Hamilton said.

"Yes, she had a cat."

Erica mentally kicked herself. What had happened to the cat? She should have mentioned something to the victim's parents. They might have wanted to take it in. She reminded herself to contact the RSPCA and make sure they kept the cat safe until the parents came to get it. She'd hate for their daughter's beloved pet to be rehomed to someone else.

"And I found some other fibres on the body," Hamilton continued, "though I believe they can all be matched to the sheets and the clothing she'd worn to bed."

"Before he stripped her," Shawn said.

"Yes, before he stripped her. There's no sign of there being any sexual interference with the body, either pre- or post-mortem."

It wouldn't be much of a comfort to the family, but it was a small blessing, at least.

• • • •

THEY LEFT THE MORTUARY, Hamilton promising to send over the written report and photographs of the body right away, and drove in their separate cars straight to the office. When she arrived, Erica found the report from SOCO had also come in.

As she read through it, her heart sank. "Shit, shit, shit."

Shawn frowned over at her. "What's wrong?"

"The flat didn't give us anything either. Not a single fingerprint from the bedroom or the balcony bars, or patio doors. He was definitely wearing gloves. No bodily fluids or hairs that didn't either belong to the victim or the bloody cat. Basically, it's given us nothing to go on."

"Shit," he echoed her sentiment.

She let out a sigh. "Exactly."

The morning passed into afternoon, with Erica eating lunch at her desk. Gibbs called a briefing for four p.m. to get an update on where they were with the case.

Suddenly weary, she rose to her feet and followed her colleagues into the briefing room. Erica took a seat near the front. Their DCI did a roll call and then looked around the room.

"Someone tell me we have a lead."

The detectives glanced around at each other.

Erica spoke up. "It's not looking good so far. The perpetrator has been meticulous about covering his tracks. The report from SOCO didn't reveal a single fingerprint or hair that didn't belong to the victim, and the pathology report didn't reveal anything other than what we already know—that she was strangled and he used his hands to do it. He stripped and positioned the body after death, and also cleaned it, removing any trace of DNA that might have been otherwise found beneath her nails if she'd fought back."

"What about CCTV from around the area? Did that give us anything?"

"It's a residential area, sir," Rudd said. "And none of the properties nearby had any kind of security cameras, so we've drawn a blank on that one, too."

"What about the neighbours?" he asked. "Don't tell me that someone scaled the front of a building and no one saw or heard anything?"

"Not that we've been able to find out," Rudd said. "It was dark, and the middle of the night. Whoever did this must be in fairly good physical shape to have climbed up onto the balcony."

He wasn't impressed by the deduction. "So, we're looking for someone who's physically fit, most likely male and young, but not necessarily either, depending on what kind of shape they're in. That should narrow it down some."

Everyone shifted awkwardly in their chairs.

"Come on, people. There has to be something! I want to know her routine, from the second she woke up in the morning to take a piss, to the last thing she thought before she closed her eyes for the night. The person who did this is most likely to be someone she knows, so I want to know every single one of her contacts, inside and out."

Erica spoke up. "We need to speak to the mother's boyfriend again, just to rule him out. It seemed the two of them didn't get on."

He pointed a finger at her. "Yes. Do that. I don't want to leave a single stone unturned. We have to find this son of a bitch."

Chapter Eight

"Looks like we're going back to Kent," she said as they left the briefing.

They were going to need to speak with Philip Reid in more detail and find out where he was the night Kerry was murdered.

Shawn nodded. "Any idea when we'll be back?"

"Late," she said. "Why? Hot date?"

He glanced away. "Maybe."

She jabbed an elbow into his side. "Good for you. Can't promise when we'll be back, though. I guess that'll depend on whether or not we have cause to bring him in for questioning."

Her phone rang, and she fished it out of her pocket and glanced at the screen.

Natasha.

Her stomach clenched. Her sister was taking care of Poppy, and her first instinct was always that something bad had happened. She wished she could put her mindset in a position where it didn't always jump to the worst-case scenario, but she couldn't help it.

"Tash? Is everything okay?"

Her sister's breath hitched, and the anxiety in Erica's stomach increased.

"Is it Poppy? Is she hurt?"

"No, it's not Poppy," Natasha said. "She's fine."

Erica allowed herself a breath.

Her sister continued, "But I've just had a call from Willow Glade, and Dad's not doing so well. They wanted me to go over there, but I've got all the kids."

"What do you mean by 'not doing so well'?"

"More confused than normal. Plus, he's got a temperature and is refusing to eat or drink anything."

Her heart suddenly seemed to double in weight, fat and heavy in her chest.

"I'll go straight over there."

"Thanks. Let me know how he is, okay?"

"Yes, of course."

She ended the call and glanced over at Shawn. "I'm so sorry to leave you in the lurch, but my dad's fallen ill. I need to go over to the care home."

"I'll drive down and speak to Reid. Do whatever you need to do."

She threw him a grateful smile. "Thanks, Shawn. What would I do without you?"

To her amusement, he blushed.

• • • •

WITHIN HALF AN HOUR, Erica pulled into the care home's carpark.

An ambulance was already outside, and she jumped from the car and ran to the entrance. She'd felt as though she'd been losing her dad, bit by bit, over the last few years, but suddenly the possibility of actually losing him hit her, and she found herself choking back tears. She didn't think she could handle going through a loss like that, so soon after losing her husband.

"Dad!" she called, pushing through the doors. "Dad?"

One of the staff stood behind the reception desk and saw her burst in. "He's still in his room. They're just checking him over."

Erica sucked in a breath and nodded, and kept going, taking the familiar route through the building to her dad's room. A small gaggle of people had gathered outside his door, and she caught the flash of the paramedics' uniforms.

"Dad?"

Monica, the care home manager, came out to greet her. "Erica, thanks for coming."

"What's happening?"

Her father's groans, peppered with several swear words, came from inside the room.

"It's okay, Mr Haswell," one of the paramedics said. "We just need to check you over."

"Where's Yvonne?" came her father's voice. "I want my wife."

Erica's heart broke, and she moved forwards, wanting him to see her. "Dad, it's Erica. Everything is okay. They're here to help."

"I don't want help. Just leave me alone." His arms—so much thinner than they'd been before—flailed.

The female half of the paramedics turned to Erica. "We're going to have to take him in. I suspect he's got a urinary infection, which often makes the dementia worse, confuses them even more, but I'd like to do some tests."

"Am I okay to ride in the back with him?"

"Yes, that's fine."

Frank tried to sit up, still trying to push the paramedics away. "I'm not going anywhere with you people."

Erica intervened. "Yes, you are, Dad. I'm sorry, but you're not well and you need some tests done."

Frank focused on her, seeming to really see her for the first time. "Yvonne? They're trying to take me to hospital."

He thought she was her mother. For once, she needed to use the mistake to her advantage. It pained her to do so, but right now, it was more important that they get her dad into hospital for tests and to make sure he got better than it was to remind him of who she was.

"Yes, Frank. That's all right. You need to go. Don't worry, I'll be right here with you." Her voice broke on the final words, and she blinked back tears.

He reached for her, and she took his hand, his skin feeling like paper, his fingers bony.

Her phone rang. It would be Natasha wanting to know what was happening, but she couldn't answer it right now. She needed to focus on her dad.

She moved to the other side of the bed to allow the paramedics to bring the wheelchair in, then she helped them to move him from the bed to the chair, where they strapped a harness around his waist. She held her breath, thinking he would fight against the restraint, but he seemed to be out of energy. They covered his lap and shoulders with waffle blankets, aware of how cold it was outside. Frank seemed to have lost his fight, and she stayed back and let the paramedics make sure they'd done everything they needed before they wheeled him outside.

"Let me know how he gets on," Monica asked her as Erica followed the wheelchair out of the building.

Erica nodded. "I will."

"Hopefully, he'll be right back again." Monica gave her a reassuring smile.

"Yes, let's hope so." But inside her head, she was screaming, *but what if he's not? What if he never makes it out of hospital again?* She didn't want to have a negative mindset, but after what she'd gone through over the past year, it was hard to stay positive. She'd experienced the worst and knew it could happen.

Outside, the air bit her cheeks, and she stood with her arms wrapped around her torso as the paramedics moved her dad onto a stretcher in the back of the ambulance. She hated feeling so useless and helpless. Normally, she was the one in charge, the one telling other people what to do, but, in this situation, she had to stand back and let others do their job.

"You can get in now," the female paramedic said, beckoning her in.

The paramedic sat with Frank in the back, monitoring his vitals, while Erica took a seat on the bench opposite. The male half of the team slammed the rear doors behind them and then went to the front and got behind the wheel.

Erica took Frank's hand as the engine rumbled to life around them. He didn't squeeze it in return, and his eyes had slipped shut.

She looked anxiously to the paramedic across from her. "Is he okay?"

"He's just sleeping. All the excitement must have worn him out."

She nodded, praying that was all it was. The ambulance didn't use the lights and sirens, which at least meant that they didn't view this as an emergency. She took some comfort from that.

Her phone buzzed again, and this time she answered it. As she'd been expecting, it was Natasha, clearly worried and wanting an update.

"Hi." Erica found herself conscious of the other woman she was sharing the confined space with. "I'm in the back of an ambulance with Dad. They're taking him in."

A sharp intake of breath came down the line. "Oh my God. Is he all right? I mean clearly he's not all right, but you know, *is* he all right?"

"They think he's got a urine infection which is making him more confused than normal. They want to run some tests. He's dehydrated, too, so they'll put him on a drip for a while and get some extra fluids into him."

"Should I come? I can get Barry to come home from work, and he can watch the kids."

"No, it's fine, really. There isn't anything you can do. How about I just give you a call if anything changes."

"Umm, yeah, okay. I guess that'll make things easier." She hesitated and then asked, "Do you think he'll be all right?"

Natasha might be the elder sister by three years, but in that moment, Erica felt like the older one, the one who needed to care and reassure. She recognised that need in her sister's voice—it was the same one that had been so present in hers after Chris died and she'd been crying on Natasha's shoulder and begging her to somehow make everything all right again. The trouble was, sometimes, it didn't matter what anyone said—there was nothing anyone could do to change the terrible things that happened in the world.

"We'll know more when we get to the hospital," she said, unable to give her sister the reassurance she needed. "As soon as I know anything, I'll let you know."

She hung up, and Erica sighed and focused her attention back on her dad. He looked much the same.

They arrived at the hospital, and she was once more swept along in a flurry of activity.

"We're going to take him through for those tests," the female paramedic said. "It might take a little while. Do you want to go and grab a coffee?"

Could she use her rank to remain in the room with him? She was tempted to, but at the same time, she didn't want to get in the way. Her dad didn't seem to know she was there, or where he was, all the activity around him not disturbing his sleep. A worm of worry twisted through her. He must be really sick not to wake up, even with being moved from the ambulance into the hospital. Or maybe he was simply exhausted from the fight he'd put up back in the care home?

"Someone will come and find you once we've got him settled."

"Okay, thanks."

She appreciated how kind they were all being. These were good people.

She waited while the paramedics handed Frank over to the hospital staff, and watched the gurney being wheeled down the hall and through a set of double doors, that opened automatically as they approached and then calmly closed again.

She helped herself to a big dollop of hand sanitiser from a box on the wall—ever conscious of the number of germs present in a hospital—and got her bearings. Her job meant she spent more time in this place than she would have liked. As a police officer, she should be hardened to it. She'd had to deal with some of the most disgusting situations. She'd been spat at, pissed on, had literal shit thrown at her, but still the hospital just made her think she was sucking in great lungs full of germs every time she inhaled. Not that the hand sanitiser could help much with that.

She found her way down to the cafeteria and queued up for a cup of crap coffee– black, two sugars—and then found an empty table in the corner.

She took in the sight of all the various people sitting around the tables and wondered what their lives were like. Some were clearly members of staff, doctors and nurses, and other clinicians, who were on a break, but others were families. An elderly couple sat opposite each other, a metal pot of tea between them. A family with a little boy around Poppy's age ate sandwiches. A woman in a suit had a laptop open in front of her. Were they visiting people, or were they suffering with illnesses themselves and were here for scans or checkups? The complexity of all these individual lives hit her. How every person had their own worries and fears, and loves and hates. Society was an intricate beast, that was for sure.

Taking a sip of her coffee, she grimaced. She shouldn't have bothered. Erica fished her phone out of her pocket and swiped to bring up her sister's name. She hit 'call'.

Natasha answered immediately. "How's it going?"

"I'm not sure. They've taken him for some tests. I'm sitting in the cafeteria drinking terrible coffee."

"So, no news yet?"

"No, sorry. I actually wondered if I could speak to Poppy quickly."

"Yeah, of course. I'll just pass over the phone."

A shuffle and a mumble, and then her daughter's sweet voice came on the line. Something inside Erica loosened.

"Hi, Mummy."

"Hi, sweetheart. How was school?"

"It was fine. Aunty Tasha said that Grandpa isn't well."

She gave a sad smile and pressed the phone closer to her ear. "No, darling, he's not. I'm at the hospital with him now."

"Grandpa's not going to die like Daddy, is he?" she said in a worried little voice.

Unlike with her elder sister, Erica found she could find the words to reassure her daughter.

"No, darling. He'll be fine. Everyone gets sick from time to time. He just needs a little more help because he's older."

"Oh, okay. Will you be coming to pick me up soon?" She lowered her volume. "I like Aunty Tasha's house, but I like our home better. It's really noisy here."

Erica found herself smiling. She was pleased Poppy still liked their house. Sometimes, she worried it was too quiet and that Poppy preferred it at Natasha's with all her cousins around her.

"I'll come as soon as I can, okay?"

"Okay. Bye, Mummy. I love you."

"I love you, too, Pops."

Poppy handed the phone back to her aunt.

"I'll call if I get any news," Erica told Natasha.

"Yes, please. I'll be waiting anxiously."

Erica ended the call.

Movement came beside the table, and she glanced up to see Shawn standing there.

"What are you doing here?" She was surprised to see him.

He handed her a decent cup of coffee. "Thought you might need this."

"Oh my God. You're the best. How did it go with Reid?"

"He was with the mother all evening, and through the night, and she can vouch for his whereabouts."

"That doesn't mean he wasn't involved. He could have hired someone or was in with someone in an effort to kill Kerry." She noted Shawn's raised eyebrow. "I know it's a bit of a stretch, but it's not impossible."

"He doesn't have any kind of record, no history of violence or assault. Other than the two of them not getting along, we've got no reason to believe he was responsible for her death."

"Shit. We still can't rule him out fully though."

He took a seat beside her. "No, we won't."

"You don't have to stay," she said. "Don't you have a hot date to get to?"

He grinned and shook his head. "Nah, I decided to cancel."

"You didn't cancel so you could come and sit in this hellhole with me, did you?"

"No," he said, but he glanced away. "I just thought it wasn't right."

"Really? Oh, that's a shame."

He shrugged. "It's fine. I probably saved her a headache. She was a bit too young for me."

Erica arched an eyebrow. "Oh?"

He chuckled. "Chill out. Not that young. She's twenty-five."

"And you're what? Twenty-nine? That's hardly much of an age difference."

"I'm almost thirty," he pointed out, "and anyway, it wasn't so much the years as the attitude. She's carefree and having fun, and I deal with all of this shit."

He waved his hand in a circle near his head, but he wasn't gesturing at the hospital. He was talking about their job and all the stuff that came with it. It was hard not to let all the horror and darkness spill out of your head and infect the innocent people around you.

She reached out and squeezed his hand, the size solid and comforting beneath her palm. "Sometimes we need that," she said. "It's like an antidote, a way of remembering that the world's not all bad. And I get it, really, I do. I feel that way with Poppy, like I'm worried she'll somehow see inside my head and be poisoned by it all, but I'd never not want her in my life."

He pulled his hand away. "I'm surprised you'd say that, after what happened with Chris."

Her chest tightened. "What happened to Chris was different."

"Was it? How can any of us truly know that our jobs won't affect our loved ones, somehow? Aren't I just being selfish by letting someone into my life when I know there might be a chance I'm putting them in harm's way?"

She exhaled a long breath through her nose. "I suppose we just have to let the other person make that choice."

Poppy doesn't have that choice. I brought her into the world without considering whether or not I could keep her safe.

Chris had always been a barrier between Poppy and the danger Erica brought home with her, but now he was gone.

Still, she could never imagine her life without Poppy in it. Being a detective shaped who she was, but so did her daughter. She needed both sides to keep her balanced. Maybe that was selfish of her, but she couldn't change things.

"Just give her a chance to make up her own mind," she continued. "That's all I'm saying."

He shrugged one shoulder, his lips pursed. "Maybe. I'll see."

She picked up her cup and pushed back the chair. "Thanks for the coffee. I'd better go up and see how Dad's getting on."

He got to his feet as well. "Do you want me to hang around?"

"No, I'll be fine, honest. Go home and get some rest, or go and call your date and tell her you changed your mind."

"Not going to happen, Swift. But nice try."

"I don't like to see you on your own all the time."

"Yeah, ditto. Anyway, I'm not on my own. I've got you." He nudged an elbow in her side.

Stupidly, her cheeks heated. He didn't mean anything by it. He was just teasing her—that was what they always did, tease each other. They'd become friends after he'd supported her during that time after Chris had first been killed, but there wasn't anything more in it than just colleagues who were close. Despite telling herself this, she didn't want him to notice her pink cheeks, so she kept her head down, her hair falling over her face.

"I'll let you know if I hear anything more about the case," he called after her, perhaps puzzled at her hasty retreat. "And call me if you need anything."

She lifted the disposable cup in a wave to show she'd heard and continued across the cafeteria, winding her way through the tables and the families who were sitting nursing their own cups of terrible coffee and stale sandwiches.

Chapter Nine

"Did you think I wouldn't notice?"

Lara froze, her wooden spoon still in the pot of tomato sauce she was heating on the hob, her fingers around the handle.

"Notice what?" she managed to reply, doing her best to keep her tone light and airy.

"Come on, Lara. Don't play these games with me. You know you'll lose."

She forced herself to continue stirring. "I don't know what you're talking about."

Alarm bells rang in her head. She was making a mistake. It would be better just to tell him the truth, wouldn't it? That she'd been helping out an old lady who had seemed to be in an even worse position than her, if such a thing were possible. But she knew why she wasn't telling him. She was frightened of what he might do—not to her, she could live with that, and had lived with that for as long as she could remember. No, it was Mrs Winthorpe she was frightened for. If Tristan thought the old lady had his money, he might pay her a visit and demand to have it back. The trouble was that Mrs Winthorpe couldn't give it back. Lara had already paid off her bills with it. What would Tristan do if he wasn't able to get the money out of her? Lara didn't want to think about it.

He took several steps closer, crossing the kitchen behind her. She remained focused on the sauce, but she was conscious of his exact position in relation to hers. Her breathing grew light and rapid, beads of sweat popping on her upper lip. She'd always known this was coming, from the moment she'd made the decision to help the old lady, but that didn't make it any less frightening.

"You know exactly what I'm talking about. The missing money."

There was no point trying to deny it. "Oh, right. That."

"That? Is that all you can say?"

"I'm sorry, Tristan. I got paid in cash, and I put it in the back pocket of my jeans, and then when I got home it wasn't there anymore. I searched the inside of the car, hoping it might have fallen out there, but I couldn't find it. Then I retraced my steps, but I think someone must have found it and kept it for themselves."

She didn't want to turn and look at him, certain he would read the lie on her face.

"Are you sure you're not stashing it away, Lara? Creating a separate little fund in the hope I won't find out about it."

She forced a laugh. "Why would I do that? I have everything I need right here."

"Don't forget everything I do for you, Lara. You wouldn't know how to exist without me. We're the same kind of people, you and I."

She understood his reason for thinking that, but that wasn't the truth. They were different—they had to be. The thought of being the same as Tristan made her wonder if there was any point at all in her being alive. Would *he* be able to cope without *her*? Would he know who he was if she was no longer around?

The crazed thought went through her head that her death would be worth it if only for him to lose his footing in life. She would be free then, and Tristan would come undone. If only she could also be around to see it.

She didn't doubt for a second that he loved her. He did. It was his own warped version of love, but it was no less real to him.

"Since we're missing money for this month due to your carelessness, you will have to make it up to me in another way."

An unseen fist reached into her guts and twisted them. "I'm making dinner, Tristan."

"I'm feeling inspired. Dinner can wait."

"But it'll get cold. It's almost done. How about we eat first?"

She wanted to buy herself some time, though her punishment was inevitable.

He leaned past her and lifted the spoon from the pot, bringing it to his lips and tasting the sauce. "Hmm. Did you use dried herbs in that or fresh?"

"Fresh, of course. I know how much you hate dried basil."

"And the tomatoes were all fresh?"

"Yes, I roasted them first."

"You need to add a little sugar to bring out the flavour."

She already had, but she wasn't going to tell him that. She hoped his distraction with the sauce was going to be enough to make him forget about how she was going to repay him for the 'lost' money. But Tristan was one of those people who never seemed to forget anything. It was as though he stored up every single thing she'd ever done wrong to use against her. Sometimes, it would be something that had happened several years ago that he'd fish up to use as proof of some misdemeanour or another.

"That can wait," he told her. "It'll taste better once it's had time for the flavours to infuse."

Inwardly, she groaned. She was hungry, and it would be hours now until they got to eat. Sometimes, he'd lose track of time, and hours and hours would pass. By the time he was done, she'd be freezing cold, exhausted, and famished.

But she wouldn't be able to persuade him otherwise.

She dropped the spoon into the pot and turned off the heat.

Then she followed him out into the conservatory and peeled off her clothes.

Chapter Ten

E mma Wilcox had been struggling to sleep ever since Ian had left.

She still didn't understand it. She thought they'd been fine—well, maybe not fine, but with the same kind of problems all couples who'd been together for more than twelve months had. Her confidence had taken a blow, that was for sure. She'd always thought he was lucky to have her, really. Long blonde hair, decent sized rack, pretty face, and it wasn't just physical either. She had a good job and paid more than her share of the mortgage and other bills. She even cooked his damned dinner for him when he got home from work—and she was a good cook, too, if she did say so herself. She was a fucking catch! But no, it hadn't been enough for Ian. He'd had to go and get involved with one of the girls from his work and decide that he wasn't in love with Emma anymore.

She hadn't been expecting it. People said when things like that happened it felt like being hit in the chest, and they were right. It had been like she'd walked straight into a brick wall and had been left stunned, with little cartoon tweety-birds or stars spinning around her head. They'd got married young, true, but to be divorced by the age of twenty-seven was absolutely gutting. If she ever started dating again—something she couldn't ever imagine doing—she'd have to tell her dates that she was a divorcee. She cringed inwardly at the thought alone.

The shame of it, the embarrassment and regret, weighed her down. She hadn't been able to bring herself to tell her parents yet, though she'd confided in a friend over coffee. She was sure Ian leaving her would go around the rumour mill soon enough. Hell, people probably already knew he'd been having an affair. They always say the wife is the last one to know.

The click of a door came from downstairs.

She sat up, her ears straining. That had been the front door, she was sure.

Bloody Ian. Had he come back? It was the middle of the night. Was he home to say he'd made a mistake and beg for her forgiveness? As much as she hated herself for it, her heart tripped in nervous excitement. Yes, that had to be it. He'd probably had a row with the little whore he'd moved in with and decided he'd made a mistake. The relief at not having to tell everyone he'd left her, at not being a divorcee in her twenties, made her head swim. She'd give him a hard time at first. She'd make him grovel, but deep down she wanted him back. Her life plan had meant that she'd be having kids before she hit her thirties, and with him gone, she'd have to start all over again. Plus, life was just easier with Ian. Who did she have to turn to when the sink was blocked up or she couldn't get a lid off a jar?

Emma jumped out of bed and ran her fingers through her hair, hoping she wasn't a complete mess. She didn't want him to take one look at her and turn around and head out the door. Her skin puckered with goose bumps, and she wrapped her arms around her. Jesus, she'd forgotten how cold it was now. Still, Ian would soon be able to warm her up. She'd just have to force herself not to think where his dick had been recently.

More movement came from downstairs. He was probably lugging his bags in.

"Ian?"

No reply came. She frowned. She hoped he wasn't going to act as though he was the one hard done by. She'd always been faithful to him. There might have been a few flirtations with other men at times, but she'd never acted on them.

"Ian, is that you?" Her voice tremored, and she clenched her fists. "Ian? Fucking answer me, will you."

A light cough, a clear of the throat. Yep, that sounded like him. Hadn't he heard her? He was probably wearing those bloody headphones that he always had clamped on his ears. She should have made him leave his house key when he walked out, but then he paid half the mortgage on the place, and she couldn't afford for him not to, so she hadn't pressed the subject. She regretted that now.

Her moment of fear was replaced by irritation, and she clomped down the stairs deliberately loudly. All the pain and anger she'd experienced over the past couple of weeks bubbled up inside her, and she discovered herself spoiling for a fight. Maybe she wouldn't let him warm her up in bed after all. Maybe she would throw him out again and tell him to go and make it up with that slut he'd set up home with. Only deep down, she knew she wasn't going to risk sending him back to her. What if she did and he decided to stay?

"Ian?" she called out again. "You'd better not—"

She reached the bottom of the stairs, and someone stepped out in front of her. A shriek of surprise escaped her lips. In the darkness, it took her a moment, the briefest flash of time, and then reality sank in.

That wasn't Ian.

The shriek turned into a scream, and she spun on her bare heels to sprint up the stairs. But the man, this stranger who had somehow got into her home, grabbed her ankles and yanked her feet out from under her. She hit the stairs hard, her chin clacking on the tread, her teeth snapping together. All the air exploded from her lungs, and she tried to suck in another breath, only for a painful wheeze to sound. Before she could even think about what to do next, he pulled her the rest of the way down the stairs, so she landed in a heap at the bottom.

He stood over her, large and towering. She lifted her arms to batter him away, but he pushed her hands to one side and stepped over her. For a second, she had the crazy idea that he was going to walk away, but then he reached down to her and his hands knotted in her hair, yanked her blonde locks into a ponytail. He walked towards her living room, dragging her by the hair. Pain shot through her scalp, intense and blinding, tears filling her eyes.

Emma screamed and kicked out, but the movement only made the pain worse and she was reduced to clutching her skull, certain he was going to yank her hair out by the roots.

They reached her living room, and he bent and hauled her back up, then shoved her so she fell onto the sofa. In only the t-shirt and knickers she'd worn to bed, her legs were bare, leaving her exposed.

"Please, don't do this. You don't have to do this."

What was it she thought he was going to do? Rape her? Kill her? Could she hope that he wanted neither of those things and was just a drug addict needing to steal something of worth in order to get his next fix?

But he seemed too strong to be a drug addict, and there wasn't that air of need and desperation around him. Quite the opposite. He seemed fully in control.

Still, she had to try.

"I've got a laptop," she babbled, pressing herself into the back of the sofa, as though she hoped the cushions might open up and swallow her. "And a mobile phone. They're both worth a lot of money. I can show you what the passwords are and everything, so you won't have to go to all the effort of trying to get them unlocked."

"Shut the fuck up," he snarled.

She clamped her lips together, not wanting to upset him. Maybe if she just lay back and let him do what he wanted, he'd leave without hurting her any further. Her scalp throbbed from where he'd pulled her hair, and her chin and jaw ached from hitting the stairs. But right now, she didn't care about any of those things, she only wanted to make it out of this alive.

A crazy idea flashed into her head. Was Ian behind this in some way? Was this a friend of his who he'd sent in here to punish her for something? Maybe shake her up enough to make her think she needed to have a man in the house for her own protection? The idea was absurd—Ian wasn't like that—and he was the one who'd left her, but she just needed an explanation, some way of making all of this understandable.

"How did you get in here? Did Ian give you the key?"

"I told you to be quiet."

He climbed on the sofa and straddled her. She'd just been lying there, frozen in fear, but now her paralysis broke, and she turned into a wildcat. She pummelled at him with her fists, bucked and writhed, and kicked. She screamed again, but his hand clamped over her mouth, stifling her. She moaned against his palm and twisted her head from side to side, trying to dislodge him, but he didn't budge. His weight pressed down on her torso, making it harder for her to inhale. Combining that with the hand over her mouth and her intense panic, she found herself growing lightheaded from the small amount of oxygen, and her initial fight seeped from her body. Then his hand moved from her mouth and wrapped around her throat, and was quickly joined by his other hand. He squeezed.

She lifted her fists to punch at his chest, but it did no good. Her world was greying at the edges.

Go for his eyes. Claw them out.

Her mind was still fighting, geeing her on, but her body didn't want to comply. As his fingers tightened further, her arms fell to her side, jerking and twitching like fish suffocating on a drying riverbank during a drought.

Was this it for her now? Would she pass out and never wake up?

And her final thought that passed through her head was how Ian was going to feel like such an arsehole for ever leaving her.

Chapter Eleven

E rica had been on her way in to visit her dad in hospital when she'd received the call from one of the detectives in Homicide and Serious Crime telling her that a body of another young woman had been found.

The second murder hadn't happened in Erica's borough. She didn't often venture to North London, and Brent Cross was well out of her way, but there was no denying the link in the two cases. The MO was clearly the same.

The detective who'd called her, DI Alex Carlton, was in his forties, with a serious demeanour, combined with a twinkle in his eye and a smile that always made Erica think he had more going on in his head than he was letting out of his mouth. She liked him, though, and was pleased he'd called her directly instead of going to Gibbs. She'd, of course, called her DCI in return to let him know what was happening, but that Carlton hadn't kept her out of the loop warmed her to him. In turn, she'd then called Shawn.

"Shit. This isn't going to be a one-off then," Shawn had said when she'd filled him in on what Carlton had told her.

"Doesn't look that way. He's got a taste for it."

"We have to figure out who this bastard is before he does it again."

She'd agreed. "Let's hope the body and crime scene gives us more than the last one."

The truth—however uncomfortable—was that they'd needed this second murder. Over the last couple of days, they'd drawn a blank on every lead, what few of them they had, on Kerry Norris's case.

She pulled up on the street behind Shawn's vehicle. He must have only just arrived, or else he was waiting for her, as his driver's door opened and his long, lean body unfolded from the car. Like her, he wore a suit with a heavy overcoat to protect against the cold, and he buttoned the front of his jacket and then slammed the car door shut. He turned to her with a half-smile. It was never easy in these situations. While it was in his nature to be friendly, someone had lost their life, and so she sensed his reservation. She could tell he wanted to ask how her dad was doing and how she was as well, but it was a private matter, and there were too many people around to talk about it.

Her dad was still in hospital. He was on a drip and antibiotics, but the doctors had reassured her he was doing well, and so she'd left to pick up Poppy, fill in Natasha about how he was, and then head home for some sleep.

The houses they approached were semi-detached, ex-council properties with front gardens that had almost all been turned into parking spaces with mid-range cars on them. One of the drives had a skip piled with rubble out the front. Remaining small patches of grass separated one driveway from its neighbour. In most other cities, these would be cheap family homes, but in London, no houses were cheap. Higher wages generally made up the disparity in property prices, but it was still difficult for people to get on the ladder unless they had parents who were happy to help them up onto that first rung.

Uniformed response cars blocked the way, but they weren't the only people present. As well as neighbours who'd emerged, curious and horrified at the death on their street, Erica recognised a few other faces.

"Press are already here," she mentioned to her sergeant. "Wonder who leaked the news of a second murder to them?"

There was a big turnout, with plenty of uniformed officers as well as the local borough's detective team. Most police hated the press, but someone could have accidentally let it slip, and once one of the vultures found out, word spread fast. She caught the eye of one of the female reporters, and a spark of recognition lit in the younger woman's eye.

"Detective! Can you shed some light on the victim? Is it definitely the same killer as Kerry Norris's? Do you have any idea who it might be yet? Were the two women connected at all?"

Erica put up her hand to dismiss her. "You can contact our media department like everyone else."

"Come on. Give me something," the reporter begged.

Shawn moved between them. "We've got work to do."

They pushed through the throng of press and local residents, flashed ID to the uniformed officers guarding the houses, and slipped under the outer cordon. They both donned gloves and protective footwear before stepping inside the house. Another officer was waiting just inside the front door, and he jerked his head towards the stairs.

"First bedroom on the right."

"Thanks," Erica said and mounted the stairs, Shawn right behind.

They entered the bedroom.

Just like with the first murder, the naked body of a woman lay on the bed. She wasn't propped up against the headboard, but instead was on her side, her hand beneath her cheek, the other draped across her stomach. Her bottom leg was stretched out, while the top one had been bent at the knee. Where the previous victim had looked as though she was sitting up to watch television, this one looked as though she could have been lying beside a lover.

An officer from SOCO was taking photographs of the room, and another moved around the body, numbering the crime scene and bagging the victim's hands. Directing them was a police sergeant who Erica didn't know, and with him was the DI who'd called her, Alex Carlton.

He caught sight of her and left the sergeant's side. "DI Swift, thanks for coming."

"Of course," she said. "You remember DS Turner?"

"Yes, I do."

The two men nodded at each other.

"What do we know about the victim?" Erica asked.

"Twenty-eight-year-old Emma Wilcox. Works as a recruitment consultant in the city. Married, no children."

"Married?" Erica checked. "Where was the husband?"

"He was the one who found her. They'd separated a couple of weeks ago, but he came back this morning to collect some belongings."

"He let himself in? He had a key?"

"Yes, he still had a key. Said he rang the doorbell first, but he'd thought she'd be at work, so then he just let himself in. He came up and found her like this."

"What did he do then?"

"He says he backed out in shock and called nine-nine-nine. He's been taken to the station awaiting a formal interview. I thought you'd want in on that."

She definitely did. "Thanks."

"What's your first instinct?" Carlton asked her. "You think it's the same suspect?"

"First instinct says yes. How did he get into the house?"

"There's a hole been cut in the glass of the back door. The key was in the lock on the other side, so it appears as though he'd just reached in and opened it."

"How is the killer getting to and from the victims' homes?" she wondered out loud. "He must have some kind of tools with him if he's able to cut the glass in the door. Let's find out exactly what he would have used and where they'd be purchased. If they're heavy, that might mean he'd be more likely to have travelled by car than by foot or on public transport."

Carlton nodded in agreement. "The lack of blood means he wouldn't get noticed just walking out of here. Assuming he was wearing gloves from the lack of fingerprints, he would have just rolled them off and either thrown them away or put them in his pocket."

"If he's thrown them away, he might have tossed them somewhere nearby." She remembered the skip on one of the driveways. "Let's get a search team on the surrounding area to look in every local bin in the area for any gloves. Plus, let's find out if there's any CCTV nearby, especially in one of the adjacent houses. We might get lucky on this one."

"We've got officers going door-to-door, see if anyone heard anything last night and if any of them have any security cameras." He continued, "Neighbours say they heard screams coming from the house during the night, just before three a.m., but they say it wasn't unusual. The couple were thought to have quite a passionate relationship, and the rumours were that the husband had been having an affair and might have left her for another woman. There were many screaming rows before this one—often during the night—and so they just chalked it down to that."

She shook her head and exhaled a sigh. "So, if the couple hadn't been having problems already, the neighbours might have called nine-nine-nine and we'd have caught the bastard in the act."

"Looks that way."

"Is it possible the husband had something to do with it?" Shawn asked. "Doesn't sound as though the breakup was amicable."

Carlton turned his attention to Turner. "It's a possibility worth exploring, but we can't ignore the similarities between this case and the Norris one. Both women are blonde, killed in their homes, currently living alone, and of similar ages. I'd put a tenner on her not having been sexually assaulted as well. My hunch is that there's something connecting the two of them and we need to find out what it is."

"Perhaps the husband was having an affair with Kerry Norris," Shawn suggested. "If he was known for cheating, there's no reason he stuck to one other woman."

Carlton glanced back to the body on the bed. "It's definitely something we need to investigate. These don't appear to be crimes of passion, though. Crimes of passion tend to get very messy, but these have been carefully thought-out, and premeditated."

Shawn shrugged. "A copycat to make it seem as though the previous killer also killed his wife?"

Erica shook her head. "There are too many details that weren't released. Unless someone actually saw that first crime scene, I couldn't see how this isn't the same person. The MO is so specific, there will be something that's connecting these women. Even if the killer thinks he's picked them at random, there's something that's drawn him to both of them. They were professional women, so let's look at where they work. Is that how he's coming across them? What else do professional women use? Gyms? Hair salons? Nail bars?"

She checked the victim's fingers, but the nails were cut short and unpolished. "Maybe not nail bars then." She scanned the rest of the body. The victim's hair was carefully arranged around her shoulders, falling over her neck.

"Do you see that?" she pointed out.

"What?" Shawn frowned.

"The hair has been pulled forward again, instead of pushed back from the face."

"You think he's done that for a reason? Why? Is he trying to make them appear more lifelike?"

"It hides the strangulation marks," she said, carefully lifting one lock of hair to reveal the brutal red lacerations and the dark-purple and blue fingerprints. There were blood bursts in the whites of the eyes as well, and the victim also had bruising around her chin.

Carlton pointed at the marks. "That might have happened before he'd managed to strangle her. There was a struggle, perhaps. She might have tried to run or fight back."

"So, there's a chance we might get something from under her nails then," Erica said.

Shawn exhaled a breath. "Not if he's cleaned this one down as well as he did Kerry Norris."

Erica shared his frustration. It was as though the killer deliberately had as little physical contact with the victims as possible. He strangled them and washed and arranged them, but that was all.

"What are you doing after you wash them and arrange them?" she asked out loud, as though hoping the killer might somehow reply.

"Was there a chair in Kerry Norris's room?" she asked Shawn.

"Yes, there was."

Erica chewed at a dried piece of skin on her lower lip as she thought. "So, is he just sitting with them."

"And then what?" Carlton asked. "He just watched them? Or did he do something else?"

Shawn shook his head. "There was no sign of any semen or spermicide in the bedroom, so it doesn't look as though he masturbated, even into a condom."

DI Carlton moved around to the other side of the bed, taking in the victim from a different angle, as though she could reveal the answers to the multiple questions they each had. "If this isn't sexual, then what?"

"Power?" Erica said. "Strangulation is a crime of power. It tends to be seen in more domestic violence cases."

Shawn pursed his lips. "We should consider that the victims knew their killer then?"

"At this point, we need to consider every possibility."

DI Carlton turned to her. "How do you feel about taking the interview with the husband? I need to finish up here, and it would be good to get a head start on that."

"Absolutely. I'll see if I can find a connection between him and the first victim, or his wife and the first victim."

Carlton nodded. "Yes, there has to be something. Nothing is ever completely random."

Chapter Twelve

E rica left Carlton back at the crime scene. Shawn went to speak with the neighbours who had heard the fighting to see what other information they could give on the couple, and if there was anything else they may have seen or heard that would help them find who was responsible.

She checked her phone for any updates on her dad, but there was nothing. She hoped he'd had a good night. She felt bad that she hadn't had the chance to visit him, and so much was landing on her sister's plate once again. It was only for a short time, she told herself. Once this case was over, she'd be able to focus on her family again. Until the next time, of course. And there was always a next time. No matter how many bad fuckers they took off the streets, there always seemed to be more to take their place.

Erica went down to the local station where the victim's husband had been taken for questioning. She explained to the desk officer who she was and why she was there, and he showed her through to the interview room.

Ian Wilcox sat with his elbows on the table, his face in his hands, crying openly. Even after Erica entered the room, he didn't stop crying, and she looked around for a box of tissues to hand to him.

"Mr Wilcox. My name is DI Swift. I'm so sorry for your loss."

He sniffed and wiped his face with the back of his hand instead of using the offered tissues.

"Do you understand that I need to ask you some questions about your wife?"

"Yes, I understand. I want to do whatever I can to find who...who—" His voice cut off, and he choked back another sob.

"I need to let you know that this interview is being recorded."

He nodded to show he'd heard.

"I'll need you to speak out loud for the sake of the recording," she said.

"Sorry. Yes."

"Can you tell me your full name?"

"Ian Charlie Wilcox."

"Date of birth."

"Seventeenth of February nineteen eighty-five."

"And your current address?"

He lifted his head at that question. "Do you want my home address with my wife or the place I've been staying?"

"Which would you currently consider to be your home, Mr Wilcox."

His lower lip trembled, and he covered his face with his hands. "I don't know anymore. "This is my fault. I could have stopped this from happening. If I'd been there, I could have protected her against the bastard who killed her, but instead I'd left her, alone and defenceless, just because I was bored and wanted something different."

"So you were no longer living at the residence where your wife's body was found?"

"No, I'd left a couple of weeks earlier. It was so stupid of me. I-I'd been having an affair, and I wanted out."

"What is the name of the woman you'd been having an affair with?"

He dropped his head, clearly ashamed. "Melanie Dickenson."

"We'll need to speak with her at some point, too, so she can verify your whereabouts?"

He nodded.

"Can you talk me through the time leading up to discovering the body of your wife?"

"Umm, I woke up about seven, took a shower, had breakfast. Mel left for work by eight, and I logged on to my laptop and answered some emails."

"What is it you do for a job, Mr Wilcox?"

"I'm in sales. Hospital equipment."

"And then after you'd checked your emails?"

"I had an appointment to get to, but not until mid-morning, so I figured I'd swing by the house and grab some more of my belongings. I only had a few bits, basically what I'd taken with me when I left, and I was running out of shirts."

"You still have keys for the house?"

"Yes, I do. I hadn't got around to giving them to Emma, and she'd never asked for them. I mean, to be honest, it didn't occur to me to give my set to her. It was still technically my house. I pay half the mortgage on it." He gulped. "I guess the house is all mine now."

Erica shifted in her seat and sharpened her gaze. Why had he said that?

He must have realised how it had come across as he sat up. "I don't mean it like that. I was just thinking out loud."

"But you do stand to benefit from your wife's death?"

"No! Well, yes, obviously the house is mine now, but if you think I'd ever do anything to hurt Emma, you're completely on the wrong track."

"The affair probably hurt her," Erica pointed out.

"You know that's not what I meant. I'm talking about physically hurting her. I've never laid a single finger on that girl. Not once, and I never would have done. I can be a bit of an arsehole when it comes to relationships, but I wouldn't hurt her like that."

"What about the other way around? Did Emma ever get violent with you?"

His eyes widened in surprise at the question. "No, never! I mean, there were some slammed doors and maybe the occasional thrown plate, but she never hit me or anything."

Erica lifted an eyebrow. "Were any of those thrown plates aimed at you?"

He shook his head. "No, honestly. It wasn't like that."

"Okay, what time did you arrive at the house," she prompted, bringing the conversation back around to the day in question.

"Around nine."

"Was there anything unusual that caught your eye? Anyone hanging around?"

"No, nothing like that. I rang the doorbell, and when I didn't get any answer, I let myself in through the front door. I called her name, just in case she might not have heard the doorbell, or hadn't been able to answer, which obviously she couldn't, but I didn't know that then."

"Then what did you do?"

"I checked the kitchen and living room, making sure she wasn't there."

"You didn't notice the hole that had been cut in the glass in the back door?" she asked.

He shook his head. "No, I didn't. I suppose I was distracted. I wanted to get in and out as quickly as possible. I felt a bit guilty for being there without Emma knowing. When I decided the house was empty, I went upstairs."

"Straight to the bedroom?" she checked.

"Yes. My shirts were still in the wardrobe. I walked into the room and saw her like that. I knew right away that she was dead."

"How did you know?"

He squeezed his eyes shut for a moment and opened them again. "It was her face. She was staring into nothing, and the whites of her eyes were all bloodshot. And there—"

He broke off.

"You were going to say something?"

He glanced down at his hands folded on the table. "It's going to sound stupid."

"Believe me, Mr Wilcox, I've heard everything. Nothing will sound stupid to me."

He blew out his cheeks and nodded. "There didn't feel like there was any life in the room. I don't know how else to explain it. It didn't feel as though I'd walked in on Emma. She was just... gone."

"And what did you do then?"

"I ran out of there and called the police from my mobile. I was shaking so hard and I couldn't bring myself to go back in the room, not with her body like that."

"I noticed there was no car in the driveway," Erica said, changing direction, keeping him on his toes.

"No, the only vehicle we had was mine, and it's a company car, so it came with me when I left."

"How did Emma get to and from work then?"

"Public transport. She normally caught the Tube."

Erica made a mental note to check the routes of the two women. If they were both on public transport, even if they were coming from different directions and parts of the city, there might have been a Tube line or station, or bus route that crossed both their paths. The killer could be another passenger, or an Underground worker.

"How long had you known Emma for?"

"About seven years. We met when she was a student and got together. We had our ups and downs, but in the end, she wanted to get married, and I went along with it. I can see it was stupid of me now. I loved her, I still do, but I was too young to be settling down like that. I wasn't ready."

"So, you had an affair?"

He ducked his head. "I know it sounds bad, especially now Emma is... you know." He seemed unable to say the word 'dead'.

"And when was the last time you saw your wife?"

"God..." He ran his hand over his head. "I'm not sure. Last Monday or Tuesday? Yeah, I think it was Monday. I came over to pick up a few bits and pieces. She looked like shit." He glanced up at his use of words. "Sorry."

Erica waved a hand to tell him to continue.

He did. "She was begging me to come back, but I told her that wasn't going to happen. The whole thing was kind of awkward and embarrassing, to be honest. I just wanted to get the hell out of there."

Erica experienced a prickle of irritation and did her best to tamp it down. Emma Wilcox had been betrayed by her husband, had watched her marriage, her whole future ripped out from under her, and all the dickhead could think was how embarrassing her being upset had been. Erica knew how that felt, to lose a husband, even if it had been in completely different circumstances, to have to reassess your position in the world and how you'd envisioned your future to be. Poor Emma had been going through all of that, and then some bastard had decided to kill her. Erica always tried not to let her personal feelings affect an interview, but seeing Ian Wilcox snotty and tearful after what he'd put his wife through because he hadn't been mature enough to tell her he was too young to get married years earlier made her want to punch something.

"When you saw her on Monday, what would you say her mood was? Did she seem frightened? Maybe mention anything or anyone unusual hanging around?"

"No, not at all. Like I said, she was upset. She was focused on me and Mel—the other woman. She was angry, understandably, and upset. But she didn't mention anyone else, or that something else was bothering her."

"Did she ever have any problems with drugs or gambling, or anything like that?"

"No, not Emma. She liked a glass of wine or two, but that was all. I've never known her to get into any kind of trouble."

"Do you think she might have started seeing someone after the two of you broke up?"

His expression was almost the same as when she'd asked if Emma had ever been violent, and Erica experienced another pang of sorrow for this poor young woman whose husband had not only left her, but who had never even considered the possibility that his wife might also be interested in someone else.

"We'd only just broken up," he exclaimed.

"That was plenty of time for you to have found someone else."

His cheeks flared with colour and pinpricks of sweat broke out on his upper lip. "That was different."

It wasn't though, and she knew she didn't need to say it out loud for him to see that.

"So, Emma hadn't met anyone else, as far as you're aware?"

"She wanted us to get back together," he mumbled, knotting his fingers together.

"I want to know Emma's routine," she said. "What were her habits? Did she go to the gym? Did she take any classes or have any hobbies that she went to on a regular basis? Where does she get her hair done? That kind of thing."

He lifted his head and jerked his chin. "She has a calendar on the kitchen wall where she writes everything down, all her appointments and nights out and stuff. I can get that for you."

"That's helpful, thank you, but I'll get one of my detectives to locate it."

"What about her social life? Does she have any favourite pubs or restaurants? I'm going to need the names of her friends, too."

"I'll write them all down for you."

"I'd appreciate it."

She had the horrible feeling this was going to go the same way as the Kerry Norris case. Ian Wilcox didn't seem to be able to tell her anything about who might have killed his wife.

Erica exhaled a sigh of frustration and prepared to go over everything again.

Chapter Thirteen

S he arrived back at the office to put together her report.
Rudd hurried to catch up, walking alongside her, the low heels of her boots clacking against the floor.

"Gibbs is asking after you. He wants to see you in his office."

Erica cursed under her breath. "Shit." She glanced towards her DC. "Any idea what he's after?"

"I assume it's about the Norris case, but not sure." She pulled a sympathetic face. "Sorry."

"Don't worry about it."

"Before you go," Hannah Rudd's eyes brightened, "I did some checking up on the victim of that second case in Brent Cross and noticed that both of the women worked south of the river, each within a walking distance of each other."

Erica slowed and turned to her. "You think that's how he's choosing them? He's seeing them at work, or walking to and from work?"

"Yes, possibly, which means there is a chance he's also working nearby."

Erica followed her train of thought. "So, he could also be a professional person? He's certainly intelligent, from the way he's left the crime scenes and how he's accessed the properties."

"Should we be warning women who work in that area?" Rudd suggested. "Especially young, blonde women?"

"It might be an idea to release something to the press, though we don't want him to know we're narrowing down the search. I'll run it by Gibbs and see what he thinks. Good work on that."

The other detective beamed. "Thanks."

Praise where praise was due. No one worked well when they felt unappreciated. She wished Gibbs understood that. Her heart sank at the likely reason he'd called her into his office. This was bound to be about her taking time off for her dad again. She wished he knew how lucky he was to have other family members he could pass off all non-work-related events onto, but it wasn't that easy for her. When Chris had been alive, she'd never been able to simply cut off her emotions and sense of responsibility from her homelife. She wasn't sure she'd even want to. What kind of person would she be if she stopped caring about the people she loved at home and let everyone else deal with family life? Her life was her family and her work. There was absolutely zero space for anything else.

She knocked on Gibbs's office door, waiting until she heard him call her in, and then entered. "You wanted to see me, sir—oh!"

They weren't the only two people in the room. A man in a suit sat in the chair opposite Gibbs. He turned towards her and rose to his feet.

"Hello again, Swift."

Gibbs cleared his throat. "DI Carlton has agreed to join forces with us on these two cases. It made sense to bring the investigation under one umbrella."

"Of course." She glanced over her shoulder to where she'd left Rudd. She hoped the presence of Alex Carlton wasn't going to cause any friction in the office. He was an attractive man, and, as far as she was aware, single.

"He's going to bring some of his DCs over as well," Gibbs said, "make sure we can cover enough ground to catch the bastard who's killing these women. I don't want another one showing up on my doorstep."

Their Violent Crime Task Force had been set up primarily to deal with the rise in knife crime but was varied enough to take on all kinds of violent crime, including murder. If they happened to be in the right borough, and the specialised homicide squads had too much on their plates, the case came to them. But they were only a small team, and they often needed help, especially in bigger cases. With two women already dead, and fearful of a third showing up any day now, she understood the reasoning to bring detectives over from the Major Investigation team. Good detectives were in short supply, and they often needed to blend resources when cases got too big for one team to handle alone.

Erica gave Carlton a smile. "Good to have you on board."

"Thanks. I hope I can be of some help. I've taken some time to bring myself up to speed with the Norris case, but it doesn't look as though you've got any solid leads. Hopefully, we'll be able to make more progress by combining the two cases."

She tried not to take their lack of progress as a personal insult, but it was hard not to feel the sting of his words.

Carlton continued, "While you were interviewing the husband, I broke the news to the second victim's family. They were devastated, of course, but couldn't give us any idea of anyone who might have wanted to harm Emma. They also weren't aware that there were marital problems and that the husband had left. I can only assume she had been hoping him leaving was only a blip and he would come back again."

Erica shook her head. "Poor woman."

"We'll have to wait for the reports from pathology and SOCO," Gibbs said, "and hope they give us more to go on than the first one."

"Whoever is doing this is planning meticulously," Erica said. "He's getting in and out, with no witnesses."

Carlton picked up a pen on Gibbs' desk and twirled it between his fingers as he spoke. "The first victim lived alone, but as far as we can tell, the second victim hadn't made it public knowledge about her husband leaving, since it was news to the victim's family, so the killer must have learned about it from somewhere as she was alone at the time of the attack."

"Or it was just luck?" Erica suggested.

"Possibly, but would he have taken that chance? Considering how prepared he seemed to be for both of the killings, not leaving any witnesses or DNA or fingerprints behind, I doubt he would have taken the risk of something like a husband being home when he broke in."

"DC Rudd has just pointed out that both of the women worked on the South Bank," she informed them. "It might just be a coincidence, but it's worth checking out."

"Plenty of professional people work in the city," Gibbs said.

"True. But at this point I think we need to cover any connection, however tenuous."

"We'll be going over all of this in this afternoon's briefing," Gibbs said. "I want to have everyone there. We'll send someone down to their places of work, speak to colleagues, find out if anyone suspicious had been hanging around, if that's how he's choosing them. And find out who knew about the couple breaking up. Even if the wife hadn't told everyone about it, someone must have known. I want both of the women's routines over the past week as well."

Erica nodded. "Yes, sir."

• • • •

IT WAS GONE EIGHT BY the time she got home with Poppy, and she was fully aware that she'd only managed to get back at that time because of the extra resources DI Carlton had brought with him. Dinner had consisted of cereal and toast, but Erica couldn't find the energy to be worried about her lack of culinary skills.

"Come on, little Miss Smarty Pants," she instructed Poppy when they'd finished. "Into bed."

Poppy pouted. "I'm not a smarty pants!"

"What? A smelly pants then!" Erica teased.

"No!" The girl collapsed into a fit of giggles.

"Little Miss No Pants?"

Poppy shrieked with laughter. "No! Not no pants."

Erica did her best to keep a straight face. "That's what you said. Little Miss No Pants."

"No! Nothing to do with pants."

"Little Miss No, then?"

Poppy was still laughing. "Not 'no' either."

"You don't want me to say no," Erica confirmed.

"Yes!"

"Little Miss Yes then?"

Poppy folded over with laughter, and Erica reached out and tickled her skinny ribs. Her daughter squealed again, and Erica joined in the laughter.

"Come on, you. This isn't going to help you get to sleep."

"More!" Poppy demanded. "More tickles."

She was tempted to give in, aware these times with her daughter were rare and precious, but they both needed to get their sleep. "No more. Time to lie down and close your eyes."

Poppy's lower lip jutted out, but she flopped down into the bed, and Erica pulled the covers up over her shoulders. She smoothed back her daughter's hair and placed a kiss on her temple. She lingered to inhale Poppy's familiar scent of shampoo and the warm toast she'd eaten before bed. If anything ever happened to this child, she wasn't sure she'd have the strength to go on.

She made sure to check the locks on the doors twice that night.

Chapter Fourteen

M ovement came from downstairs.

Lara sat up in bed and frowned. Someone was definitely down there. The only other person in the house was Tristan, so she had to assume it was him.

She glanced at the digital clock. 3:27.

What on earth was he doing up at this time? Maybe he couldn't sleep? Or perhaps he'd heard something and gone down to investigate.

There wasn't much chance of her getting back to sleep without finding out what was going on. With a sigh, she swung her legs out of bed and reached for her dressing gown on the back of the door. Feeling cosier and safer with its soft folds wrapped around her, she opened the bedroom door and stepped out onto the landing. At the top of the stairs, she paused again. They always left the downstairs hallway light on during the night—a subtle way of announcing to any potential intruders that there were people home—and that hadn't changed, but it didn't look as though there were any other lights on downstairs either.

Another noise came from down there.

They didn't have any pets. Tristan always insisted that all they did was make a mess. He didn't want to have to pick up some animal's shit or find hair in his food. Lara found herself agreeing with him, but it was only half-hearted. She understood his need for everything to be perfect, for their home to be spotless, for not a single thing to be left out of place, and a pet would never be able to abide by his many rules.

But deep down, she longed to have something else in the house that she could love unconditionally, and who would love her in return. She dreamed of having a warm, furry creature she could cuddle on her lap. She'd have loved a dog or a cat, but at this point would even settle for a rabbit or a guinea pig, but it would never happen. Once Tristan made up his mind on something, there was no changing it.

She crept down the stairs, her heart feeling as though it was in her throat. She wasn't sure why she was creeping—this was her house, after all. She just had the sense that something was going on that shouldn't be. At the bottom of the stairs, she turned left and crossed the dining room and into the kitchen. Beyond that was the conservatory Tristan used as an art studio.

She paused. Sure enough, the studio was in full light. On the other side of the easel, she could make out Tristan's shoulders, his knees spread, and bare feet planted on the floor. Jesus Christ, was he naked? What the hell was he doing sitting painting in the middle of the night with no clothes on?

A strange knot of dread twisted inside her. What should she do? Should she confront him and ask him what he was doing? Was the painting the same one as he'd been working on that afternoon, when she'd been posing for him? If so, why was he working on it now, and why was he naked? It was January, and the house was hardly warm—quite the opposite. How was he not freezing sitting there? The conservatory was a particularly cold spot, though it was like a furnace in the summer. Did he have one of the electric heaters plugged in? She couldn't see from her position, though she hoped he did. He'd catch a chill otherwise. Already the cold from the floorboards was leaching up through her soles, and she wished she'd taken the time to put on her slippers as well.

No, she was thinking too much into it. She couldn't fully see that he didn't have any boxer shorts on or anything, and really this was his house, so if he *was* naked, he was within his right to be. It didn't mean he was doing anything weird or perverted. He was an artist. He was supposed to be somewhat eccentric—which he certainly was. This was a new quirk, though. Or maybe it wasn't. He might have been doing this for ages, she simply hadn't noticed that he'd got out of bed before.

Trapped in her indecision, Lara bit on her lower lip until she tasted blood. She wasn't going to confront him, was she? As much as her gut told her that something wasn't quite right about this situation, she'd do whatever she could to keep attention away from herself and not start a fight. After the incident with the missing money, she couldn't risk upsetting him further.

She took a step back, and then another, retracing her path. She wanted to know if he'd seen her and wouldn't be able to tell if she turned her back on him. When she left the room and was back at the bottom of the stairs, she allowed herself to relax enough to face the direction she was going. Moving cautiously, aware of which stairs creaked and what floorboard clunked when too much weight was pressed on it, she made her way back to the bedroom. She closed the door behind her and climbed back into bed, pulling the duvet up over her shoulders.

Though she'd worn her fluffy dressing gown the entire time, she discovered she was chilled to the bone. Even now, huddled up under her duvet, the mattress still warm from where she'd vacated the bed not long before, she shivered, her teeth chattering together.

What was Tristan up to?

Lara huddled herself tighter into a ball and willed for sleep to return.

Chapter Fifteen

Before going into the office that morning, Erica had taken it upon herself to drive down to the South Bank and walk the route between the offices of the two victims. Though it was early, the area was already busy, filled up with people in suits, takeaway cups of coffees in their hands, walking at a determined march. She glanced into the faces of every man she passed, wondering if he could be their killer. Any who were older and appeared unfit, she quickly dismissed, remembering the athletics it would have taken to get onto the balcony at the first victim's home, but that didn't narrow things down much.

Her phone rang, and she answered. "Swift."

It was DC Rudd. "Sorry to bother you so early, but a man has come into the station. He says he knows who killed those two women."

It wasn't unusual to get people who insisted they had information on a murder, especially when the deaths had made the news and no one had pointed a finger at a suspect yet. They received multiple phone calls from people saying they had information. On the odd occasion, the person actually did know something that would help the case, but for the most part, they were simply people who wanted to feel like they were involved, or else wanted to make trouble. Often, the same names or variations on names came up over and over again.

"Can you not deal with him?" Erica asked.

"I'm sorry, but he's saying he'll only speak with you."

"Have you run a check on his name? Is he already known to us?"

"Yes, I have. He's not one of our repeat offenders, and other than a speeding ticket three years ago, his record is clean."

Erica sighed. "What feeling are you getting from him? Does he seem genuine?"

"I'm not sure. He's serious, but it's always hard to tell."

"You can't get an initial interview out of him?"

"Nope. He's refusing to say anything until you get here."

"Shit."

She was tempted to leave him waiting, but what if he had something vital to tell her and he changed his mind? They currently had no definite leads, and the thought of letting one just walk out of the station door twanged uncomfortably at her insides.

"Okay, fine. Make him wait in the lobby until I arrive. I'll be there in half an hour."

Letting out another sigh, she ended the call and headed back to her car.

• • • •

ERICA PAUSED IN THE corridor outside the interview room and peered through the square of reinforced glass in the top panel of the door. Upon her arrival, the man had been brought to an interview room, and was now waiting for her.

"Do you want me to come in with you?" Rudd asked her. "We don't know if he's going to be violent. He's been searched and doesn't have any weapons on him, but you can never be too careful."

"Are you okay to wait outside? I'm sure he'll be fine, but just in case."

Her constable nodded. "I'll be right here."

The man sitting on the other side of the door was in his mid-twenties, with a pair of wire-framed glasses sitting on his nose, his light-brown hair in tight curls. His shirt was rolled up at the sleeves and open at the collar, exposing a small crucifix against his skin. Religious, then? Or was that just a piece of jewellery that meant nothing to him?

Erica straightened her jacket and put back her shoulders then opened the door. The man barely reacted to her entrance, just the hint of a smile touching his lips.

He tilted his chin in a nod. "Detective Inspector Swift. Thank you for coming to speak to me." He was softly spoken with a posh accent. Public school boy?

"Of course. Thank you for coming in, Mr...?"

"Mr Dunsted. Aaran Dunsted. I hope the other detective wasn't offended when I said I only wanted to speak to you."

Erica gave a tight smile. "It takes a lot to offend us, Mr Dunsted. My time is very limited, however, so I'd appreciate it if we could get on with this. I'll be recording our interview." She didn't ask if that was okay. She was recording it, whether he liked it or not.

He gestured with one hand. "Please do."

"Interview with Aaran Dunsted, conducted by DI Swift in interview room three." She added the time and date and then turned to the man sitting opposite.

"I'm sorry about what happened to your husband, Detective."

Immediately her senses sparked a warning. Was that why he was here, and why he insisted on speaking only to her? He was here because of some morbid curiosity to meet the detective who worked on the Eye Thief case, the same one whose husband was murdered by the man she'd been trying to catch.

"Thank you, but I assume you're not here to offer your condolences. You told DC Rudd that you have information on the murders of Kerry Norris and Emma Wilcox."

"Yes, I do. I know who killed them."

She lifted an eyebrow. "You do? Who?"

"I did."

Erica sat back in her seat. "You're confessing to the murders of Emma Wilcox and Kerry Norris?" She was understandably sceptical.

"I am."

"Tell me about them. About the women. About the way they were killed. Why should I believe you?"

"I strangled Kerry Norris in her bed. She barely woke up before I managed to wrap my hands around her throat, and then I squeezed until she stopped breathing, and I did the same to Emma Wilcox."

Anyone could have found out the women had been strangled. It had been all over the news.

She took a different tack. "Tell me a bit about yourself, Mr Dunsted. Your date of birth and current address?"

He reeled them off.

"Are you married? Any children?"

He scoffed slightly at the possibility. "I'm only twenty-five, DI Swift. Plenty of time for all that."

Not if you're behind bars serving two life sentences for murder there won't be.

She kept her thoughts to herself. "Of course. And what do you do for a living?"

"Graphic design. Not as interesting as it sounds, I'm afraid."

He knew his way around a computer, then.

"Is that in the city?"

"Yeah, South Bank."

The same area of London where the two women had worked.

Erica nodded and wrote it down. "I see."

Though the interview was being recorded, she found it was good to get her own thoughts down while they were happening.

"Why are you here, Aaran?" she said. "What's made you want to confess?"

"I want you to stop me. I don't want to do it again."

"If you wanted to be stopped so badly, why did you leave the crime scenes so clean? You must have realised that a lack of DNA evidence would have made it harder for us to connect this to you."

"I didn't know at the time that I wanted to stop."

"So why the change of heart? You're telling me that two days ago you had no intention of being caught and went to the utmost effort to hide any possibility of linking you to the crime and all of a sudden you've changed your mind?"

"I'm sure changing one's mind isn't only a woman's prerogative. I'm allowed to change mine, too, aren't I?"

His tone was sly, and she didn't like it.

In her experience, killings like this didn't usually result in a suspect willingly confessing. There were certainly people who did confess, when they were being interviewed by a clever detective who was able to get into their heads and uncover the emotional reasons behind the murders. But this didn't feel emotional to her, quite the opposite.

"Back to Kerry Norris," she said. "What about her dog? What did you do to the dog?"

She was trying to catch him out in his lie.

One side of his mouth curled in a smirk. "Kerry Norris didn't have a dog. Are you trying to play games with me, DI Swift?"

"I don't know, Aaran," she deliberately used his first name. "Are *you* trying to play games with *me*?"

He pushed his glasses higher up his face. "Kerry Norris had a cat. Skinny, annoying little thing. I would have killed it, too, but it hid behind the sofa and I didn't have the time to waste to dig it back out again."

He was right. Kerry had had a cat, but wasn't that something he could have found out online? It was hard to keep things a secret these days. There might have been pictures of it on Kerry's social media. What woman with a cat didn't post pictures of it online these days? Even though, of course, all the detectives and police officers and SOCO who investigated the scene knew everything was confidential, there was always the chance one of them was friendly with a local reporter, or who had a wife or husband who grilled them with details that they could impress that week's book club or bowling meeting with. With no DNA found in the victims' homes that they could link him to, he needed to spill the details to prove he was the real killer, but she couldn't give him hints about what needed to be said.

"Mr Dunsted, at this point I'm going to offer you a solicitor before we proceed any further. I also wish to advise you that you do not have to say anything, but it may harm your defence if you do not mention when questioned something which you later rely on in court. Anything you do say may be given in evidence."

He waved away her words with a sweep of his hand. "I don't want a solicitor. I already said that the only person I'm willing to speak to about this is you, Detective. And I'm fully aware of my rights."

She wished he'd taken the solicitor—it would protect them both when it came to a conviction—but she couldn't force him to.

"Very well. What did you do to Kerry after you'd killed her?"

"I didn't need to do anything to her, Detective. I'd already done what I needed. She was dead."

"So, you didn't do anything to her body?"

"I'm not a pervert, if that's what you're implying."

Neither of the bodies had been sexually assaulted, so he was also right on that account.

"How are you choosing your victims? What connection is there between them?"

He shrugged. "No connection. I saw them in the city and followed them. It was completely random."

"What was it about them that caught your attention?"

"Pretty. Smartly dressed. Looked as though they had good jobs." The corner of that smile again. "A lot like you, Detective."

She didn't rise to the comment. "How did you know that they both lived alone?"

"It's easy enough to find those things out. Everything is online these days. Once I found out where they lived, everything else fell into place."

"But Emma Wilcox had only just separated from her husband. That information wasn't online." He would already know this since the news had already been widely reported.

"I found her on social media. Her account isn't private. She'd posted an angry rant about how her husband had been fucking someone else, and even tagged him in it. She deleted it shortly after, but not quickly enough to stop me from seeing it."

Erica made a note to check this. She already had their tech team going over both women's social media accounts. Would they be able to track down a post that had been made and then deleted? Her understanding of how social media worked wasn't great.

"What time did you go to the women's homes?"

"I broke into the first victim's house just before two in the morning, and the second was around the same time."

Erica did her best not to let her thoughts show on her face. Emma Wilcox's neighbours had said they'd heard a scream closer to three a.m., but they could have been wrong.

"Both of the women were asleep when I found them," he continued. "It was easy to kill them, disappointingly so." He smiled, and Erica's heart grew cold. "I'd have preferred them to put up a bit more of a fight."

She thought of something. Emma Wilcox had been found with an injury beneath her chin. It was assumed it had happened during the struggle, but there was always a chance she'd done it before going to bed that night. Or she might have got up to use the bathroom during the night and knocked her chin then.

"Emma had an injury in a certain place. Can you tell me about that?"

"It was dark in the room, Detective. How was I supposed to notice every little thing?"

"It was dark the whole time?" she queried. "You didn't turn on any lights?"

"And get noticed? Why would I risk it?"

"You just said that you wanted to stop killing, and that's why you're here. Maybe that would have been enough of a reason."

Why would you arrange the bodies if you couldn't see them? She didn't say that, though. She didn't want to feed him any more information than he must have already garnered from the news reports and online articles.

She scribbled in her notepad: 'were the bedroom lights left on or off?' If they were off, it didn't mean he was telling the truth, of course. The real killer might have switched them on when he was in the room with them and then turned them off again when he left.

"How did you get into the buildings?"

He folded his arm and smiled. "Really, Detective, don't you think you should ask a harder one than that? I cut a hole in the glass of the doors and let myself in that way."

He could have checked the outside of the victims' homes, she realised. Now the investigators had been and gone, there was no one watching the buildings to ensure no one went near them. He would have been able to figure out how the killer got into the buildings from there. But no one other than the detectives working on the case had seen the inside of the crime scene, the position of the bodies.

"Excuse me for a moment," Erica said. She spoke out loud for the sake of the tape. "DI Swift is pausing the recording for a break." She looked back to him. "Can I get you anything while I'm gone? Coffee? Water?"

He sat back and folded his arms, appraising her. "No, I'm fine. Take as long as you like. I'll be right here."

Erica pushed her seat back and turned and left the room. Rudd was leaning up against the wall, but she straightened as Erica stepped out.

"How's it going?" Rudd asked.

"If he's not the killer, he's done plenty of research into the victims and the crime scenes."

"You know what these kooks can be like. Some of them can be pretty resourceful."

"Yeah, but he doesn't seem kooky." She pursed her lips. "I don't know, but it feels like he's watching me, trying to figure me out somehow."

"An attention seeker?" she suggested.

"Quite possibly, but I can't rule him out yet."

"What do you think we should do with him?"

"SOCO have released the last crime scene so I'm thinking of taking him there. I want to see if he knows the layout of the house, and the route the perpetrator would have taken to reach the bedroom. And if he can tell us the position the bodies were found in, I might start to take him seriously. If not, we'll know he's spinning us a story."

"Want me to get some backup? I can get a couple of uniformed cars to accompany you."

"I don't think he's dangerous, and he's not under arrest yet, but tell Turner he'll be coming with me, and have a patrol car accompany us as well."

Rudd nodded. "When do you want to leave?"

"Tell them thirty minutes."

"Yes, boss."

The DC turned and walked back down the corridor towards the office.

Erica looked back through the window. Aaran Dunsted still sat in exactly the same position as she'd left him, reclined in his chair with his arms folded. She didn't like how calm he was. Was this really the man who'd murdered Kerry Norris and Emma Wilcox? Could she picture him breaking into their homes and pinning them down on their beds, his hands around their throats? Then he stripped them down and washed their bodies with sponges and towels from their own bathrooms, and then arranged their bodies as though they were posing for him. He'd have committed them to memory to go over and over, to feed upon like a fucking vampire until the memory was no longer fresh and he had to do it again.

He would know the positions he'd left the bodies in.

Chapter Sixteen

E rica parked the pool car across the empty driveway of the
Wilcox property. As far as she was aware, Ian Wilcox had
remained at his new girlfriend's and hadn't moved back in here.
She didn't know how much of that was because he'd decided he
was happier with the girlfriend, despite his apparent grief and
regret in the interview room, or if he'd simply not been able to
bring himself to live and sleep in the house where his wife had
been murdered. It wouldn't surprise Erica if the place went on
the market in a few months, Ian Wilcox happy to cut all ties to
his now dead wife, and his former life.

Behind her, the patrol car containing Aaran Dunsted
pulled over. He was cuffed in the back, with two uniformed
officers in the front. Instinct told her that Aaran wasn't
dangerous, despite his claims, but she still hadn't wanted to risk
it only being her and Shawn who brought him here.

It had taken them a little while to locate the keys to the
Wilcox property from evidence. She'd left Aaran Dunsted in
the interview room, happy to let him sweat for an hour. But
when they returned to cuff him and take him out to the patrol
car, he'd still been sitting in the same position and barely
seemed fazed at all by the extended wait. Most people would
have started to get restless, pacing around the room or
knocking at the door to find out what was going on, but he'd
remained almost preternaturally still. When she'd gone back
into the room, he'd acted as though she'd been gone for five
minutes instead of over an hour.

Shawn craned his neck out of the passenger window, looking up at the house. "You think he'll be able to tell us anything only the killer would know?"

She opened the driver's door and climbed out. "That's what we're here to find out."

She sensed curtains twitching, the neighbours wondering what the police were doing back here. This might not be the poshest part of London, but the people who lived here were just normal working families or older couples, and things like one of their neighbours being murdered by what was now a serial killer didn't happen every day. She bet people would be drinking out on their version of the events of that night for some weeks and months to come.

The two officers got out of the car behind and then opened the rear door for Aaran to join them. He did so, straightening and turning towards the house.

She studied Dunsted's reaction. He gazed up at the building and sucked in a hitching breath, a little colour flushing to his cheeks. Considering how calm he'd been so far, this was the closest he seemed to have come to having any kind of emotional response to anything. Was that because all the memories of the last time he was here were coming back to him, or was it that he was imagining what had happened in there?

"This way," she said.

She went up to the front door and unlocked it.

Shawn turned to the police officers. "It's up the stairs."

"Wait a minute, Turner," she said. "I believe Aaran here should show us exactly which route he took."

Aaran gave her that cold smile. "You won't catch me out, Detective. I'm telling the truth. And I can't show you which route I took from the front door, because I broke in through the back."

"Very well. But you can show us exactly which room was Emma Wilcox's bedroom, though, can't you?"

He ducked his head in a nod. "Of course."

Though she hated that he might be taking pleasure in walking through a murdered woman's home, she moved back and let him through. His arm brushed up against hers, and she stiffened in response. Bastard.

He took the stairs slowly. The whole house had already been worked over by SOCO, or she wouldn't be letting him anywhere near it. She could feel him sucking up the atmosphere, though, and enjoying every second of it, and she wished there was a different way she could either prove he was lying or telling the truth.

He reached the top of the stairs and paused. Erica held her breath, anticipating which way he would go. If he went the wrong way, she'd know he was lying. But he took the right, and she jerked her head at Shawn and the other officers, and they all followed him up the stairs.

Aaran paused in front of what had been Emma Wilcox's bedroom door. He'd chosen the right room without hesitation. The door was shut, and he glanced back to Erica.

"I can't open it."

Of course, his hands were cuffed behind his back.

Erica stepped forward and opened it herself. She didn't wait to allow him in first, but instead entered the room and walked up to the bed, but then turned her back on it. She didn't want to give him any idea of what she was looking for, though the news reports had said that both women had been found murdered in their beds.

Aaran followed, Shawn and the other two officers close behind. Aaran stopped beside her.

"Show me," Erica said to him. "I want to see exactly what position Emma Wilcox was in when we found her."

He jangled the metal around his wrists. "You're going to need to uncuff me if I can put my arms in the same position I put hers."

She nodded at one of the officers, who unlocked the cuffs. The officer took them away, aware that the metal could be used as a weapon if Dunsted decided to try something.

Aaran rubbed at his wrists.

Erica deliberately kept her gaze away from the bed. "Show me."

He went straight to it, climbing onto the bare mattress.

"I left her like this." He lay on his side, his hand beneath his head, his arm across his stomach, in an almost exact replica of how they'd found Emma Wilcox.

Shit. So he was telling the truth.

Aaran seemed to sink deeper into the bed. He let out a long sigh of satisfaction, and his tongue sneaked out of his mouth and lapped across his lower lip, leaving a wet trail of saliva. He was having a physical reaction to lying in the same spot a murdered woman had been found. She made the unfortunate mistake of glancing down over the front of his trousers, and her stomach flipped. Yeah, he was definitely having a physical reaction.

She curled her lip in disgust and jerked her head towards the two uniformed officers. "Get him the hell out of here."

They stepped forward, dragged him off the bed, and cuffed him again.

"Take him back to the car."

"I told you it was me," Aaran said, half over his shoulder as he was pushed from the bedroom by the two uniformed officers. "Why would I lie about something like that, Detective?"

She didn't give him the satisfaction of a response. She needed him to be out of her space so she could think about what had just happened. Outside, the patrol car door slammed, and she pictured him back in the rear seat.

Shawn lifted an eyebrow at her. "You think he's telling the truth?"

"How else would he have known unless he was the one to do it?"

Shawn pursed his lips and shook his head. "It's still not physical proof."

She ran her hand through her hair. "We don't *have* any physical proof. That's the problem. All we've got is this arsehole's word."

"Are we sure the killer didn't take any kind of memento from the women's homes?" Shawn checked.

"Not that we can figure out. None of the family or friends reported anything missing, but if it was something small and personal, they might not have noticed. We'll need to get a warrant to do a search on Dunsted's home in case he took anything there, but if he had something physical and he's trying to show us that he's the one responsible, I don't know why he wouldn't just give that up."

"He might not want to," Shawn suggested. "If he really does want to stop killing, he could still hand himself in while wanting to keep whatever memento he took."

"True." She stared around at the room again, her hands planted firmly on her hips, wishing the walls could give up what they had seen. "I don't know why this doesn't feel right."

• • • •

IT DIDN'T TAKE LONG to get the search warrant.

DI Carlton met them at Aaran Dunsted's flat. "I hear we've got a confession," he said. "And he was able to show you what position we found Emma Wilcox's body in."

"Yes, but I'm still not completely sold on him being the killer."

"Gibbs is pushing for an arrest."

She pressed her lips together. "I don't know. It's still too soon, in my mind. Let's see what his flat reveals first, if anything. Did the reports come back on the body and from SOCO?"

He nodded. "I've spoken to Dr Hamilton down at the mortuary. He agrees that it's the same killer. Just like the first victim, the body was cleaned up post-mortem, and SOCO weren't able to get any prints or bodily fluids from the second crime scene either."

She rubbed her hand across her mouth. "See, that's what's bothering me so much. Why go to so much effort to cover your tracks, only to walk into a police station within days and confess everything?"

Dunsted had even handed them the key to his flat to allow them to do the search, so they didn't need to break in. The flat was on the ninth floor of an old seventies tower block, and the lift had smelled faintly of urine as they'd waited for it to deliver them up here. Shawn had a camera to take photographs of the outside of the flat, including the address, and then to photograph anything of interest inside as well. She had the search warrant case containing evidence bags of all sizes, among other things, and she opened it up to hand out the gloves and shoe coverings for them all to wear.

Erica used the key to let them in. "Let's work clockwise," she told the other two detectives. "That way we won't miss anything."

"Do we know what we're looking for?" Carlton asked her.

"Anything that might have been taken from the two victims' homes."

They entered the property and got to work. It was small and run-down, and it didn't take more than a few minutes for Shawn to open the door onto what appeared to be the bedroom.

"Swift, you're going to want to see this."

She left what she was doing and joined him, Carlton close behind her.

She stopped in the bedroom doorway. "Jesus."

The walls were covered with newspaper clippings. She spotted the murder cases she'd worked on, and her guts twisted as her eyes locked on Chris's face peering out from between them. She fought every instinct to walk up to the wall and tear that particular clipping down.

Carlton folded his arms across his chest. "He's certainly got an interest in murder cases. There appear to be a lot of the ones you've worked on, too, Swift."

"Yes." She spoke between gritted teeth. "I can see that."

Shawn looked between them. "Does this mean he's more or less likely to be our killer?"

"Seems to me like he's had a thing about DI Swift," Carlton said. "And he used the killings as an excuse to get close to her."

"I *am* here," she said, unable to hide her irritability. She didn't like that she might have been played, or that an arsehole like Dunsted might have fooled her. She also hated that he had a picture of her dead husband in his bedroom. "Let's get all of these bagged up. They might be evidence."

It took them some time, but eventually, they had everything photographed and bagged. As she was leaving the flat, Natasha called her mobile, and she dragged off one of the protective gloves to answer.

"Everything okay?" she asked.

"Dad's being released from hospital today," her sister said. "Would you be able to pick him up?"

It was good news that Frank was on the mend, but she couldn't leave everything now. "I'm sorry, Tasha, but I'm swamped with work. I can't."

"I can't either."

"Won't the hospital arrange transport for him?" she said. "Or maybe the care home could pick him up? You could call Monica and ask."

"I thought you might do it, since you haven't made it in to see him." Her tone had stiffened.

"Sorry, but you know the case I'm working on." She dropped her volume so she wouldn't be overheard. "It's not the sort of thing I can just drop at a minute's notice."

The truth was that she didn't want to take any risks in pissing off Gibbs. She hadn't liked the way DI Carlton and her DCI had been cosying up together. She didn't want to make any mistakes right now. Carlton wouldn't be after her job, would he? She couldn't see why he would be. It wasn't as though it would be a promotion. He was coming from Homicide and Serious Crime, so it would barely be a sideways move. Something had bothered her, though, and she couldn't seem to get it from her thoughts. Could it be because of how high profile the cases she'd worked on lately had been? Was he after some of the limelight? It wasn't as though she wanted it for herself. He was welcome to it, but that didn't mean she wanted to give her boss any reason to replace her.

Natasha gave an exasperated sigh. "Fine, I'll sort something out. Just don't forget your family needs you as well."

"I know that, Tasha. It's not something I'll ever forget."

Chapter Seventeen

A hand, hot and dry, clamped over her mouth and nose. Victoria Greg lurched from sleep. She tried to sit up in bed, but the hand covering her face hadn't been from a dream or a nightmare, as she'd been thinking, but was very real. And the hand wasn't only a hand. It had a strong forearm attached to it, and somewhere beyond that, a set of shoulders, and a torso, and a pair of legs that were currently sitting astride her, pinning her down.

Panic took over. Someone was in her room—in her flat! He was on her bed and had straddled her while she was sleeping, and now had his hand over her mouth to prevent her screaming.

Victoria yanked her head from side to side and flailed around, trying to dislodge him. But the man above her seemed as immovable as stone. In the dark, she couldn't make out his features, just the general shape of his mouth and nose, and the hollow pits of his eye sockets.

His hands moved from her mouth to wrap around her throat. No, this wasn't happening, this couldn't be happening.

She was close enough to the edge of the bed, perhaps partly from the position she'd been sleeping in, but also because she'd managed to wriggle slightly to one side with him on top of her, to be able to reach down the side of it, between the bed and the bedside table. Her fingers touched smooth wood, and her heart lurched.

She'd bought the baseball bat partly as a joke. She'd been out shopping with her girlfriends and had seen the bat in a novelty shop—one of those places that sold random shit from arts and crafts, to kitchen ware, to gardening gear—and she picked up the bat and weighted in her hand, giving her opposite palm a couple of smacks as though testing it out. "This is just what I need," she'd laughed. "Who needs a stinky dog or a man to keep me safe when I can have one of these bad boys?" She'd stashed it beside her bed, a little relieved to have it, though she never would have admitted it out loud to anyone. *A woman in her early thirties, with no boyfriend on the horizon, never mind a husband and kids, was always seen as something of a pariah. What was wrong with her?* she could see people thinking. Some of her friends were divorced by now and onto their second marriages, and she hadn't even managed it the once yet.

She curled her fingers around the smooth wood and tightened, just as the intruder's fingers had tightened around her throat. She was running out of time. Her lungs burned, and her eyes bulged from her head.

Victoria Greg picked up the bat and swung it with all her strength at the side of the man's head.

The crack of the bat hitting his skull was like a gunshot, and immediately his hands vanished from her throat and the weight of him left her body.

Coughing and gasping, Victoria dragged herself to sitting. Her eyes had filled with tears, blurring her vision in the already dark room. Where was he? Where had he gone.

Then she saw movement beside the bed.

He'd fallen in the gap between her bed and the door. Already he was groaning and sitting back up, his hand clutched to the side of his head where she'd hit him. She hesitated, frozen with indecision. She should hit him again, but the bat had already fallen from her hands. In her panic, she'd dropped it as soon as it had hit his skull, hating the way it had felt, not wanting any connection with the wood, the feel of it in her hands filling her with horror and revulsion that she'd been forced to actually hit someone with it. Besides, it was one thing hitting someone in the moment, without really thinking about it, but it was another actually going on the attack. She wasn't tough or strong. He'd just wrestle the bat from her hands and use it to beat her, instead. Should she try to get past him to get out of the door and run for help? The room was only small, and she'd literally have to step within arm's length to get by. He could easily reach out and grab her again, and then the small advantage she'd had would be lost.

She glanced behind at the window. Or should she take her chances and climb out of the window and jump to the ground? She lived on the first floor, so the drop was significant, but if she was able to lower herself down slightly first, she could reduce the distance.

Another groan came from behind her, and the heavy shifting of movement.

He was coming.

She didn't have any more time to waste. If she was going to do this, she needed to do it now. Even if she broke both her legs, she'd still stand more chance of survival than if she stayed in the room with this fucking bastard. She had no doubt that he was going to kill her, but before he reached his goal, she'd probably end up wishing she was dead anyway.

Two choices. Take her chance with him or take her chance with the ground.

The ground won.

Not wasting another second, Victoria lunged for the bedroom window. Her fingers caught the handle, and she yanked on it a couple of times, her terrified, confused mind not processing why it wasn't opening. But then she saw the tiny key sticking out of the lock. Shit, it was locked.

A thin whine of terror escaped her throat. She fumbled the key, the metal feeling too thin and precarious between fingertips that now felt fat and swollen and like they didn't belong to her at all.

A growl and a thump came from behind her.

Panicked, her breath coming hard, she threw a glance over her shoulder. He was on his feet now, using the side of her bed to keep himself upright.

She turned back to the window, twisting the key, a part of her certain everything was against her and that it would break off in the lock. But miraculously, the lock popped open and, all of a sudden, she was able to throw open the window. A blast of icy cold air hit her face, but she didn't have time to worry about catching a chill.

He was coming.

Victoria swung her leg up onto the sill, hooking her foot out of the window and then pulling the rest of herself up and over, so she was straddling the frame.

Don't look down. Don't even think about it. Just do it.

If she gave herself time to consider the distance she had to jump, then she would end up chickening out. And she couldn't chicken out. If she did, she'd be dead.

She hauled her other leg over the top, so she sat in the window. Across the street, one of the houses had their lights on. The people on her road were just continuing with their lives, most likely sleeping soundly, unaware that a woman was fighting for her life only a matter of a few doors away. But perhaps that one person who struggled with insomnia might be awake, lying in bed and scrolling through social media on their phone, or perhaps had given up on trying to sleep and instead had decided to come downstairs to make a cup of tea and watch some television until they were able to sleep again.

Or perhaps someone had simply forgotten to turn off a light before they'd gone to bed, and the whole world was sleeping and unable to help her.

"Help!" she screamed, praying someone would hear her. "Someone he—"

A solid smack struck her across the back of the shoulder, like a block of stone had been slammed against her. She barely had time to process what had happened. One moment, she'd been sitting on the windowsill, and the next she was falling.

The ground came up to meet her in a split second.

She hit it with even more force than she'd been hit from behind. An ear-splitting *crack!* resonated through her entire body, inside her head, encompassing her soul and the very essence of who she was. She'd broken bones upon impact, lots of bones. She didn't feel any pain, though, which was strange. Was she dead already? The possibility almost felt like a relief.

She tried to process what was happening, but she didn't seem able to keep any of her thoughts together.

Had a door opened across the street? Or was she dreaming now?

He'd hit her with the bat and knocked her out of the window. Fuck. Why hadn't she kept hold of it? He would be coming, wouldn't he? On his way to finish off the job, perhaps to bash in her skull with her own practical joke of a bat.

A shout. Someone from across the street? Was that real? Perhaps it was just wishful thinking. No one was coming to help her. The man in her room was going to kill her...

No, she was wrong about that, too. He wasn't going to come to kill her because she was most likely already dead.

Chapter Eighteen

The excitement in the chilled air was palpable and, despite the painfully early hour—the sun had not yet deemed to cast its first wintery beams across the city—the street was a hive of activity. Uniformed response units blocked the road, while officers questioned the neighbours who'd emerged from their homes to see what was going on.

Carlton and Shawn stood in front the house, inside the outer cordon, looking up at an open, first-floor window.

Damn it, Erica thought as she approached. Now they'd *both* managed to get there before her. She wasn't in a position where she could just drop everything the moment the call came through that there had been a third attack. She'd needed to take Poppy to Natasha's before coming here.

"You know what this means?" Shawn twisted to face her. "Either Aaran Dunsted isn't responsible for the murders of those other two women, or else we have a copycat."

There was a possibility this event wasn't linked to the other two victims, but Erica suspected that was highly unlikely. Victoria Greg was blonde, thirty-one years old, and she lived alone. She fit the profile on every level, except for one difference.

She was still alive.

Erica joined the two men. "The way he screwed this one up might mean it isn't the same person."

Shawn raised both eyebrows. "Or the victim just got lucky."

"She's unconscious in hospital," DI Carlton said. "I'm not sure how lucky that is."

Shawn snorted. "She's alive, isn't she?"

"Do we know *how* she's still alive?" Erica asked.

Carlton pointed up. "She escaped through her bedroom window, but we haven't been able to talk to her yet. She was unconscious when the uniformed officers reached the scene. She's broken multiple bones, according to the paramedics, though whether that was from the fall or because she was attacked beforehand and then thrown from the window, isn't clear yet. One of the uniformed officers went with her in the back of the ambulance, but we haven't heard anything more."

"Jesus Christ." Erica shook her head, picturing how terrified this poor woman must have been. "Any idea how he got in yet?"

"The house is divided into a couple of flats with the victim owning the upstairs one. The intruder must have climbed onto a small flat roof extension out the back and cut a hole in the glass of the hallway window. The key had been left in the lock on the other side, so the intruder was simply able to reach through and unlock it, then climbed through."

"Similar way to the other two break-ins then." She didn't need to elaborate on which other break-ins she was talking about. The murders of the other two women were all over the news. Even someone not connected to the police force would have known what she was talking about, never mind another member of the Met.

"Yes, almost identical," he agreed, "with the exception of which types of entryway he used."

"What about the downstairs neighbours? Didn't they hear anything?"

He shrugged. "They weren't in. We haven't been able to locate them yet, but they might just be away."

She cocked an eyebrow. "In January?"

"People do go on holiday in January," he said.

She thought of Lucy Kim and reluctantly agreed.

This was their first real chance to get something substantial on this guy. It had been dark and they had no idea if the attacker had been wearing any kind of face covering, but there was the possibility the victim could give them a description if or when she woke up.

"A neighbour across the road heard a shout around three in the morning," Carlton continued. "He said it was distinctively a shout for help. He looked out of his bedroom window, which faces directly onto this house, and first saw that this one was standing wide open, which was unusual considering how cold it is at night at the moment, and then he saw the victim lying on the ground."

"Where is the neighbour now?"

"He's been taken in for interviewing."

They all helped themselves to protective outerwear and entered the property, taking the stairs up to the first-floor flat.

A police sergeant was in the bedroom with SOCO, and he came over to speak to them.

"Detectives, thanks for coming."

Erica nodded. "Of course. Have you found anything of interest yet?"

"We're still working the scene, but we believe it's the same person who murdered the other two women. This one got lucky."

Erica's gaze was drawn to the open window. "Do you think the victim jumped or was pushed?"

The sergeant shrugged. "It's hard to know for sure unless she wakes up and tells us, but we know that it's not in his usual MO to kill his victims by pushing them out of a window—"

"Assuming this is the same person we're after," Erica interrupted. "We don't know for sure yet. It might be a copycat. That he's been going after professional blonde women has been all over the news."

"We've never publicised how he's been breaking into the properties in the first place," Carlton interrupted. "It's unlikely someone accidentally chose to break in the same way."

Erica slowly crossed the room, trying to put herself in the victim's place, to recreate events in her mind. "The victim woke up after he'd broken in. He must have been blocking the door, because she clearly thought the window was her only escape route. She ran over, opened it, and shouted for help." Erica frowned as she thought. "Why didn't he just stop her? He wouldn't have stood by the door, blocking the exit, just to watch her go to the window and open it and call for help."

She studied the window the victim had either fallen or jumped from. It was divided into three equal sections, with the two sections on either side openable, while the frame in the middle was solid. She noticed something about the opposite side, the side which still remained shut. There was a small key in the lock. She checked the side the victim had opened. Sure enough, there was an identical key.

"Look at this. The victim didn't only open the window. She also had to unlock it first. How long would that have taken her?"

Shawn caught on to her train of thought. "Not long, but long enough for her attacker to have stopped her. So why didn't he?"

She pointed a finger at him. "Exactly."

"Could she have barricaded herself in with a piece of furniture?" Carlton suggested. "Maybe she heard him breaking in and coming up the stairs and she slowed him down that way."

"Possibly." Erica crossed back over the room to the side with the door. There was no lock on the bedroom and no sign that it had been bashed in to gain entrance. She checked the carpet for indents where a recently moved item of furniture might have once been standing, but everything appeared to be in its rightful place. "But that would mean the attacker pushed or watched Miss Greg fall and then instead of running, took the time to put the piece of furniture back in its place. There also aren't any signs of damage to the door on the other side."

"Something else slowed him down then." Shawn rubbed his wrist across his mouth. "Something the victim might have done to him before running to the window."

She liked where he was going with this. "You think she might have injured him badly enough to buy her some time?"

He locked eyes with her. "I think it's possible, yes."

A bubble of excitement swelled inside her. "Then we could be looking for someone who's recently been hurt. I'm going to go to the hospital and see if anyone has come in with any unusual injuries, and we need to get some more units covering the other hospitals in the area as well. It's not likely, but it's worth checking. Hopefully, I'll be able to get some good news on the victim's condition at the same time."

Shawn nodded approvingly. "Let us know how you get on."

Chapter Nineteen

Lara walked into the kitchen and drew to a halt. Tristan was standing at the kitchen counter, his head bent over a plate containing a couple of pieces of toast, the butter dish and jar of marmite standing next to the plate. But it wasn't his breakfast that had caught her attention—as much as she loathed marmite. It was the dark rivulet of blood that ran from his left ear and trickled down his neck.

"Jesus, Tristan! What happened to you?"

"What?" He shot her a glare of annoyance. "Nothing."

"But... but your ear. It's bleeding."

He lifted his hand to the side of his head and brought back his fingertips, tinged with blood. "Shit."

"And the top is all swollen," she continued, still concerned. "You can't have not noticed?"

"I banged my head on the cupboard door. It was stupid of me. I should have closed it. But it's not a big deal, Lara. I'm fine."

"You don't look fine. You must have really knocked it. Don't you think you should get it checked out by a doctor."

"No!" he snapped. "I told you I was fine."

She'd only been trying to help. She was worried about him. He'd woken up this morning in the worst mood she'd seen him in for ages. She didn't understand it. When he'd gone to bed the previous night, he'd been in a great mood. He'd cooked dinner with the radio on, poured her a glass of wine, and danced around the kitchen. He hadn't glanced at his easel or mentioned her sitting for him, which was always a massive relief. She'd gone to bed the previous night rather tipsy on the wine, and she'd fallen asleep the moment her head had hit the pillow. She should have known better than to accept that second glass from him, since wine always left her groggy-headed the following morning, but she hadn't wanted to break whatever good-mood spell he'd been under.

It seemed the spell had certainly broken overnight, however. Had it been injuring himself that had caused this dark cloud to hover over him? She could understand how that would have pissed him off.

"Tell me what you need me to do," she said, desperate to veer him away from the black cloud hanging over him. "How can I help? Do you want a tissue? A plaster? A cold cloth, maybe? What can I do?"

"You can leave me the fuck alone, Lara. Why do you have to be so clingy? Always asking questions. Always wanting to know everything. I'm allowed to have a life without you in it."

She reared back as though he'd slapped her. *Like you do to me, you mean.*

"I know that, Tristan. I wasn't trying to poke into your life. I just saw you were hurt and I wanted to help."

He picked up the knife and stabbed at the butter, squishing it into a distorted shape without actually scooping any of it up to put on his toast. "I don't want your help. I thought I'd made that clear. I don't need anyone's help."

She found her gaze fixed on the knife in his hand, the way he stabbed and cut and smoothed and spread. What had happened? She didn't believe for one second that his bloodied ear was caused by hitting it on a cupboard door. Something had happened, something he clearly didn't want to talk about.

Normally Tristan was so calm, restrained even when he was angry, which was often more frightening than if he just let his real feelings out, but now she found herself wishing for the more restrained version of Tristan back.

She took a step backwards, her gaze still glued on the way that knife was making such a mess of the butter.

He suddenly spun to face her, the blade—blunt, but still terrifying—pointed in her direction. "Don't you go saying anything to anyone about this."

"About what?" She had no idea who he thought she was going to be talking to.

"About this." He gestured to his bloody ear, which he still hadn't done anything about. "It's no one's business but my own."

"I-I won't tell anyone. I promise."

"You'd better not. I mean it, Lara. Keep your fucking mouth shut."

She took another step backwards. He wouldn't hurt her, would he? He loved her. He frightened her, though—he always had, in a way.

"I have to get to work," she said, her voice small.

"Maybe you should stay home today."

"What? Why?"

"The world is a dangerous place." His eyes narrowed. "It's safer here. We could both stay home. You could sit for me awhile."

The last thing she wanted was to spend all day doing that. "I have my customers expecting me, Tristan. I can't just not show up."

"That's not what I'm suggesting. You can phone them and tell them you're not going to be in."

Panic rose inside her. Her work was the one and only thing she had that Tristan wasn't involved in. Though she handed over her income each day, he didn't interfere with her while she was working. It was a pathetic iota of freedom—on her hands and knees scrubbing other people's toilets—but it was still freedom.

She thought quickly. "I won't be able to get hold of them. One of them is a doctor and they'll be at work."

He scowled. "I assume he has a mobile phone."

"*She* does have a mobile phone, but she'll be in surgery so wouldn't be able to answer. Besides, I have no reason not to go. I'll be fine."

He looked as though he was going to keep fighting her—Tristan was used to getting his own way—but then his shoulders slumped, and he turned his back on her again and refocused on his breakfast.

"Fine, do whatever you want. It's your life."

She hesitated, a part of her wanting to tell him he was right and that she would stay home with him, but if she did that, she might never get to leave the house again. She'd be trapped. And she didn't want to let her clients down. She'd always prided herself in her work—it was the one thing she'd created all by herself—and she couldn't let him take that away.

"I'll see you later then."

She backed out of the room, aware that the blood in his ear had already started to dry and turn darker. Her natural instinct was to take care of him, and she wanted to tell him to clean himself up, and to phone her if he felt dizzy or got a headache, but she didn't want to give him the chance to change his mind and insist she stay.

All of her cleaning products and equipment were always kept in the boot of her run-down old car, unless she needed to put some cloths through the washing machine, so she only needed to shove her feet into her boots and grab her coat and car keys, and then she was out of the house, hurrying down the icy driveway. Her windscreen was frozen over as well, and her heart sank. It was going to take ten minutes of the engine running to defrost it enough to be able to see out of. Every second that went past was another opportunity for Tristan to come running out of the house to snatch the keys out of the ignition and demand that she stayed.

She opened the car door and slid behind the wheel. Plugging the key into the ignition, she turned it. She held her breath for a moment, half expecting the old car to refuse to start on the cold morning, but the engine grumbled to life. She still had the ice to deal with, though. Inside the vehicle, she was surrounded in a frosty white curtain and she couldn't see out of any of the windows.

Had Tristan followed her out? Was he standing at the open front door, the butter knife still in his hand, watching her every move? Or had he come out farther than that, and was actually standing on the pavement beside her, hidden by the frosted pane?

In a moment of panic, she quickly wound down the driver's window, allowing her to see out. But there was no sign of Tristan, and the front door was still firmly shut.

She moved her attention back to the frozen windscreen. She cranked the heat up on the car blowers, thinking it was going to take her forever to get the ice cleared. But she'd left later than normal, and the pale winter sun had been strong enough to weaken the bond of the ice on glass, and as she flicked on her windscreen wipers in the hope of dislodging it, the ice rippled and squashed together, clearing a space in the glass.

Lara exhaled a sigh of relief, nudged on the indicator, and pulled away from the kerb. She was already running late.

She glanced into the rear-view mirror as she drove away, certain Tristan would come after her, either running down the street, or she'd see his car trailing hers, but there was nothing. It wouldn't have been unusual for her to have seen him following her. Now that he wasn't, she didn't know how to feel. Relieved? Or more anxious than ever?

Chapter Twenty

If there was one thing she hated about her job, it was having to spend so much time at the hospital. She could handle just about anything when it came to blood and guts and violence, but actual sickness was a whole other thing. Maybe it was because you could see blood and guts, and knew how to avoid it, but you couldn't avoid a bacteria or virus. They just lurked around in the air or on surfaces like little invasive aliens just waiting to strike you down.

Her other reason for hating hospitals was that other than giving birth to Poppy, there was never a happy reason for coming to one of them. It was always because someone was hurt or sick. People probably looked at her and wondered how she could bring herself to do her job, but she felt the same way about doctors and nurses. Maybe they actually hated illness as much as she did, and this was their way of fighting back, in the same way Erica believed her job was about fighting for those who were made victims.

She stopped off at the Emergency Department to enquire about anyone who might have come in with unusual injuries over the last few hours, but other than a toddler with a temperature and an elderly lady who'd slipped in the bathroom, their department had been surprisingly quiet. Erica had been hoping for a man in his twenties or thirties who had come in with a broken nose or something similar, but even if Victoria Greg had injured him badly enough to need treatment, he still could be hiding away, aware the police would be asking questions.

Erica remembered the way to Intensive Care from previous visits but still found herself checking the signs on the walls to double-check. All the corridors in this place looked the same. She passed other visitors and patients being wheeled on gurneys, and white-coated doctors and nurses. A few gave her nods and smiles of acknowledgment, but most ignored her.

Erica stepped onto the ward, helped herself to a hefty dose of hand gel, then located the reception area for Intensive Care. She showed her ID to the nurse behind the reception desk, who rose to her feet to show her to the correct room. A police officer had ridden with the victim in the back of the ambulance and remained with the victim, not only so they'd be able to make a note of anything that she may have said that would help them find who'd done this to her, but also for her protection. Whoever had attacked Victoria Greg might know that she'd survived and decide he should finish the job.

Memories swept over her. She'd been in this exact spot for the Eye Thief case, when she'd come to interview the first victim, who'd sadly later committed suicide. The chain of events had been life-changing for her, and her heart picked up pace, a rising panic that she needed to get a hold on. In her job, she couldn't allow herself to be shaken by cases, even when she *was* so personally affected.

"I'll get a doctor to come and speak to you," the nurse told her.

"That would be great, thanks."

Erica let herself into the victim's room.

Victoria Greg's appearance shocked her. Each of her limbs were in a cast, her neck in brace. A tube protruded from her chest, and more tubes ran into the back of her hand. An oxygen mask covered her face, and a bandage was wrapped around her head. Beside her, machines beeped and pumped fluids and oxygen and medication into her to keep her alive.

"Jesus Christ."

The officer sitting with Victoria Greg was a woman in her fifties. She had bleached blonde hair with a heavy fringe, a stocky build, and a stern expression. She got to her feet, that stern expression softening.

"I'm PC Scott," she said. "You are?"

"DI Swift," Erica introduced herself. She looked to the woman in the bed. "How is she?"

"She was in surgery all morning. She only came out an hour ago and has been unconscious ever since. She's going to be in for a long recovery."

"Did she say anything in the ambulance on the way here?"

"No. She was barely conscious then either. I'm not surprised, considering her injuries." PC Scott shot the victim a sympathetic smile, though Victoria Greg couldn't see it. "She must have been in a horrific amount of pain."

"Did we manage to get any record of her injuries before she went into surgery?"

Scott nodded. "Our forensics team took pictures of her injuries when she was brought in. Her hands were bagged at the scene, so if there was any DNA beneath the fingernails, we'll have got that, too."

"That's good. He'd cleaned the previous bodies, so we've been unable to get any samples from the other victims. She could be incredibly important when it comes to finding out who did this."

A light knock came at the door, and a man in his thirties entered. Instantly, Erica stiffened but then caught the name tag. Dr Lundy. One of the doctors here. She forced herself to relax. The suspect would be an idiot to come here so soon after the attack, knowing there would be police around. But perhaps he was worried his victim would wake up before he got here. There was a chance that she knew him and would be able to name him.

"DI Swift." She offered the doctor her hand. "How's the patient?"

He shook it. "Dr Lundy. She's stable, for the moment, but has been through a lot. A broken rib caused a hemothorax, and one of her lungs collapsed."

The doctor was young and handsome, all dark hair and thoughtful expressions. Even noticing that he was attractive filled Erica with guilt. Chris was never far from her thoughts, and she couldn't imagine a time where she would not feel guilty about being attracted to another man. Would that ever go away?

"We really need her to wake up. This was the third attack, and both the previous two victims died, taking everything they knew with them. If Miss Greg wakes up, she might be able to tell us who did this to her. There's a chance she knows the person responsible, and even if she doesn't, she may still be able to give us a description."

He shook his head. "I'm afraid I can't promise that happening. She has swelling on the brain, which is why she's being kept sedated. She also has multiple breaks to both legs, a fractured pelvis, and a dislocated shoulder. She has bruising across the top of her back, which may have been sustained before the fall, since it doesn't look as though it's consistent with the other injuries."

"You think there might have been a struggle?"

"Yes, it's possible. It definitely looks as though she's been hit by something across the back of her shoulders."

"Looks like he might have pushed her out of the window. Good thing he did, too."

"The one who got away," he said grimly. "Though if she pulls through, it's going to take her months to recover, psychologically, as well as physically."

"She was lucky."

Twin lines appeared between his dark eyebrows. "I read about those other cases in the news. Do you have any idea why the killer didn't finish the job this time? Assuming he knew she'd fallen from the window, he didn't come after her, so what happened to stop him?"

"That's what we're trying to find out, though we suspect it was because a neighbour across the street heard her calling for help."

PC Scott stepped in. "I was there when he first spoke to us. He said he'd woken up to use the bathroom and heard the shout. When he looked out of the window, the victim had already fallen, or been pushed, from the bedroom window and was lying on the ground. He ran straight out and got his wife to call an ambulance and the police, and then stayed with her until we arrived."

"She was lucky he spotted her," the doctor said. "If he hadn't, she might not have made it until morning."

It was cold, reaching the minuses on some nights.

"If there are any changes in her condition," Erica said, handing him one of her cards, "can you let me know?"

He nodded. "Of course."

There was nothing more she could get from the victim while she was still unconscious. She'd be better off interviewing the key witness, the neighbour who'd heard the victim shout for help and then found her.

The witness who'd effectively saved Victoria Greg's life.

Chapter Twenty-One

The man sitting on the other side of the table in the interview room was in his late fifties to early sixties. A grey t-shirt peeped out of the V-neck of his navy-blue jumper. He still had a full head of dark-grey hair and he rubbed together a pair of large, well-worn hands.

"Mr Renee?"

He looked up from his hands and nodded.

Erica took a seat opposite. "Thank you for coming in. My name is DI Swift. I assume you know why you're here?"

"It's because of being the first person to reach that poor woman across my street."

"Yes, that's right. Can you just tell me your full name and date of birth for the sake of the recording?"

He rattled them off.

"Are you married, Mr Renee?"

"Yes, I am. Have been for almost twenty-five years." He puffed out his chest, clearly proud.

"Congratulations," she said with a smile.

"Thanks."

"Do you have children together?"

"Yes, two boys, but they've both left home. The eldest is twenty-six, and the younger one is twenty-three. They come home occasionally for visits, but they have their own lives now. You know what they say about a son only being a son until he finds a wife. Not that either of them are married, but the eldest is settled down already."

"And what's your address?"

He told her that as well. As she'd already known, it was the same road where Victoria Greg lived.

"How long have you been at that address?"

He pinched his lips together as he thought. "God, must be about fifteen years now. Yes, definitely fifteen years."

"Do you know how long Victoria Greg's been your neighbour?"

"Not long, I don't think. People are always coming and going in the street, so I can't say I note down their moving-in dates all the time."

"Just a ballpark is fine."

He screwed up his face. "Maybe a year or so."

"And how well did you know her?"

He shrugged one shoulder. "Only enough to say good morning to, or ask when bin day was, or complain about parking on the street... that kind of thing. I don't think we've ever had a real conversation."

"What about people coming and going from her flat?"

He screwed up his face and looked as though he wanted to tell her what he thought she'd want to hear, but then blew out a breath. "No one I can remember sorry. I wish I could be of more help."

"That's okay, Mr Renee. You're doing great. How about over the last month or so? Any strange vehicles or people?"

He shook his head and glanced back down at his lap. "Not that comes to mind."

She offered him a smile and straightened her shoulders. "Let's go back to yesterday, before you'd gone to bed. What did you do?"

"I went to work, came home, had dinner and a glass of wine with the wife, watched some TV, and went to bed. It was a normal day."

"But you were up in the night?"

"It's the old bladder. Doesn't seem to hold anything these days. I'm up every couple of hours in the night, and it's not much better during the day. When I have to go, I have to go."

"You should probably see your GP about that," she suggested.

He sniffed. "Yeah, I already have. He gave me some advice about fluid intake before bed and said he can put me on some tablets, but I'm not going to start taking something at my age. I'm only fifty-eight. I could end up taking them for another thirty years, if I'm lucky enough to live that long."

"Right." She didn't know what else to say to that. "Getting back to the incident, you said you were already up?"

"Yes, and I'd already had a piss, thank God, or it would probably have ended up all down my boxers. I heard the shout and thought it might just be kids messing around, but something made me check out of the window. The other house is right opposite ours, and I noticed the bedroom window was wide open first, and then I saw the poor woman on the ground."

"When you noticed the window was open, did you see anyone standing in it? Perhaps looking out?"

He shook his head. "No, sorry. It was dark. I could see the window 'cause the movement from the fall must have made the security lights at the front of the house come on, and the first thing I thought was that it was strange the window was wide open when it was freezing outside, and I couldn't remember seeing it open like that when I went to bed. Then I noticed the bundle on the ground. It took me a minute to realise it was a person—the eyesight is going the same way as the bladder lately—but the minute I did, I forgot that I was only in my boxers and I shouted out to the missus to phone an ambulance and I ran down the stairs and straight out the front door. I didn't even care that I was half naked and it was close to freezing. All I could think was that there had been an accident and someone was badly hurt. It didn't occur to me at that point that there might have been something more sinister going on." He waved a hand between them. "I mean, I knew about those poor women being murdered, but the idea of something like that happening right on our street didn't enter my head."

"You didn't see anyone else then?" Erica asked. "No one running from the house?"

"No, I didn't, but all my attention was focused on the woman. I thought she might have been trying to open or shut the window and had lost her balance and fallen. I certainly didn't think she'd been pushed, or had jumped." His brow furrowed, creating deep ridges, and he leaned slightly towards her, across the table. "Do you know which it is yet? Did she jump or was she pushed?"

"I'm afraid we most likely won't know that for certain until she wakes up."

He gave a nervous laugh. "I might not have been quite so gung-ho if I'd known there was a serial killer lurking around."

"I'm sure Miss Greg will be happy that you were. If you hadn't seen her and come running, she might not have survived the night."

His eyes widened. "You think he would have finished the job?"

"I meant more because of her injuries and lying all night in near freezing temperature."

"Oh, right. Of course." He seemed a little embarrassed that he hadn't thought of that option.

Erica got back on track. "When you reached Miss Greg, did she say anything, or try to say anything?"

"I'm not sure. She kind of groaned, but I couldn't be sure if it was just a noise or if she was trying to tell me something. I was shouting back to my wife as well, telling her that we needed that ambulance right away."

"Did you try to move the victim at all?"

He shook his head. "No. I'd seen on TV shows that you shouldn't move someone who's been in an accident, or you might make things worse. I could tell she had broken bones because of the way her legs were at weird angles, and I didn't want to hurt her."

"You did the right thing," she assured him.

"Thanks, I hope so. Poor woman. I can't imagine being that frightened that I'd try to jump out of a first-floor window." He pressed his lips into a thin line and exhaled a long huff of air through his nostrils.

"Yes, it must have been terrifying for her."

He folded his hands on the table. "I don't know what's got into people these days, thinking they can go around attacking innocent young women like that. You just don't expect it, do you? It happens on the news and such, but you would never think that kind of thing would happen on your own street."

"No, I guess you don't." She brought them back on track. "What about over the last couple of days. Did you see anything out of the ordinary? Any strange cars driving by or people lurking around?"

"No, nothing like that. I wish I could tell you more, but honestly, up until the early hours of this morning, I thought we lived in a peaceful neighbourhood."

"Okay, thank you for your time, Mr Renee. We'll be in touch if there's anything else."

"Anything I can do to help, just let me know."

Chapter Twenty-Two

A week had passed since she'd last been to Mrs Winthorpe's house and helped to pay her bills. The old lady had told her that she couldn't afford to keep paying Lara, but Lara didn't feel right abandoning her to manage by herself. Though Tristan wouldn't be pleased about her giving up her time for nothing, especially when she could be doing something for him, her conscience niggled at her.

Tristan was at work, and she hoped he wouldn't be following her today, but even so, she found herself glancing over her shoulder, half expecting to see his car vanishing around a corner.

It bothered her that he hadn't made more of a fuss about the missing money, however. Perhaps that was the thing that niggled her. Why had he let it go so easily? It confused her. She'd still had to give him what he wanted, but once that debt had been paid, he hadn't brought it up again. She'd expected her punishment to go on for days. Normally, he would have treated her to days of silence and withdrawal, barely acknowledging her existence, but not this time.

Lara reached Mrs Winthorpe's front gate and pushed it open. It was rusted and stiff, and she had to lift it slightly to close it behind her again.

She went to the front door and pressed the bell. The ringer *ding-donged* inside the house, and Lara waited for Mrs Winthorpe's shout of "One minute!" that normally followed, while she tried to push herself out of her armchair to answer the door. On a regular day, she'd have just let herself in, but she'd left her key here the previous week.

But no noise came from inside.

Lara frowned and pressed the bell again. Perhaps the old lady was asleep and hadn't heard it the first time?

Once more, she listened out for the sound of her ex-client moving around inside the house, but there was nothing.

"Mrs Winthorpe?" Lara switched ringing the bell to knocking on the door. She didn't know how she thought that was going to help, but it was all she could think of. "It's Lara, Mrs Winthorpe. Are you in there? Is everything all right?"

Flutters of worry plucked at her heart.

She left the front door to go to the lounge window where she cupped her hands to the sides of her face and tunnelled her vision against the glass. It took her a moment to focus, but then the inside of the lounge came into view. Everything was just as it normally was, with the exception of Mrs Winthorpe not being in her chair. She hadn't fallen asleep, then? Lara checked the floor in case she'd had a fall and couldn't get to the door, or even a phone to call for help, but she wasn't there either.

Lara's concern mounted. What if she'd fallen somewhere else in the house?

She moved to the other side of the front door, where the window offered a view into the kitchen. Peering through that window as well, she did her best to catch sight of her customer.

"Mrs Winthorpe?" she called out again. "Are you okay?"

Maybe she should go and knock on one of the neighbours' doors and see if anyone had seen her.

She remembered how women in the city were being attacked in their beds. What if the same person who'd killed those women had hurt Mrs Winthorpe as well?

She shook the thought from her head. She was being ridiculous. Some serial killer who liked young, blonde women wouldn't be interested in a woman in her eighties.

It was more likely that Tristan was the one who would hurt her.

The thought stopped her in her tracks.

Hurt *her*, or hurt Mrs Winthorpe?

Lara had felt as though his reaction to her not bringing home that day's money hadn't been right. Could it have been that he'd known she'd paid Mrs Winthorpe's bills and had decided to take things into his own hands? He might have returned to the house and demanded the money from the old lady instead? She didn't have that kind of money—that was the whole reason Lara had paid in the first place—and wouldn't have been able to give it back to Tristan. What if she'd refused and he'd hurt her?

Picking up her pace, she rounded the side of the house, letting herself in through the gate into the back garden.

Would Mrs Winthorpe have a spare key hidden somewhere? Under a plant pot, or mat, perhaps?

Lara searched under the pots.

Bingo!

The key looked as though it had been there awhile, covered in a scattering of woodlice and ants and embedded in mulch. She brushed them off and picked it out of the dirt. She hoped it would still work.

She paused a moment, the key at the lock. The thought of discovering a body, poor Mrs Winthorpe having been beaten or worse, filled her with dread. Could she smell anything?

Her heart thumped. How would she handle it if she went inside the house and discovered a body? She'd seen her parents' bodies after they'd died in a car accident. Tristan had been there, too, of course, and had handled most of what had needed to be done to identify them, but it hadn't been easy. It had been them, but also not them, as though she'd been looking at a waxwork version of their poor battered bodies. Her mum had gone straight through the windshield, and the doctors said the head injury would have killed her. The seatbelt had been frayed so that it snapped on impact. Her father's seatbelt had held, but it hadn't helped him at all. His side had struck the tree, the metal warping around the trunk. The fire service had needed to cut his body from the frame of the car.

Lara gave her head a shake. She needed to stop thinking about that. It had happened almost eight years ago, and she told herself things were better now, but still sometimes it hit her like a truck. Especially around days like Mother's and Father's Day, where their absence was felt more keenly. They'd left the house she and Tristan now lived in, and there had been enough money to keep them going. Tristan had never really got on with them, but he wouldn't say anything bad about them now they were dead.

She realised her thoughts had vanished back into the past again. Was she deliberately putting off opening the back door? Maybe. She took a breath and turned the key, a part of her hoping it wouldn't work, but it did, and the door swung inwards.

"Mrs Winthorpe? It's Lara. Are you okay?"

To her relief, the house didn't smell any different to how it normally did—a little musty, perhaps, but that was all. Lara stepped through the kitchen, keeping an eye out for anything unusual. Could Tristan really have come here and threatened an old lady? He was cruel to Lara, but did he have it in him to put the frighteners on her customer in order to get her money back?

Movement suddenly came at the front door, and Lara sucked in a breath and froze.

It's Tristan! He's followed you here and will make you pay just like he made poor Mrs Winthorpe pay!

The front door opened, and Lara gaped in surprise. Even more surprised was Mrs Winthorpe at finding her cleaner standing in her entrance hall.

"Oh my God, Mrs Winthorpe, you're okay!"

She had to hold herself back from hugging the other woman.

"Of course I'm okay. I just popped to the shop for some milk." She seemed genuinely baffled about finding Lara in her home. She held up an old-fashioned crocheted bag containing a small one-pint plastic bottle of milk. "What on earth are you doing here?"

Lara was stupidly relieved to see she was okay.

"I clean for you today, Mrs Winthorpe. When you didn't answer the door, I was worried something might have happened. I went around the back and found a spare key under a plant pot to let myself in."

"I'm so sorry if I gave you the wrong idea, Lara, dear, but you don't need to clean for me anymore. I thought I told you that I couldn't afford to pay you. I didn't think you were coming, which was why I'd popped out."

Lara was flustered now, feeling silly and like she'd overstepped her mark. "Oh, yes, of course. I did know that. I just didn't want you to be left unable to cope, that was all."

"You're a sweet girl, you really are, but honestly, I can manage. Your time is important, too. I don't want you wasting any of it on me. You've been too kind as it is. Go and find yourself a proper customer who pays *you* instead of making you feel so guilty you end up paying her bills for her."

"It wasn't like that, Mrs Winthorpe. I just wanted to help."

"I appreciate that, but now I can help you by sending you away. I promise, if my financial situation changes, you'll be the first person I call, both to pay you back that money and to get you back in to work, but for the moment, I'm going to have to let you get on with things."

"Okay, Mrs Winthorpe. As long as you're sure you're all right."

The old lady gave her another smile. "I'm fine, all the better for what you did for me last week. Now, get along, and find yourself a paying customer instead."

Lara nodded and stepped past her and through the open front door, back out into the cold. "Better close this. You're letting all your heating out."

"Will do, dear. Bye now."

"Bye."

And the door shut behind her again, leaving Lara standing out on the street, wondering what the hell had just happened, her mind racing. She truly had believed something awful had befallen her customer—her ex-customer now—and that Tristan had been behind it.

Was she the one who needed her head checked, or was the man she was living with truly dangerous?

• • • •

BY THE TIME SHE GOT home, she'd managed to push her thoughts about Tristan possibly hurting someone out of her head.

She got in to find him sitting at the dining room table. The radio was silent, and he didn't even have his phone to scroll through. He was just sitting there, waiting for her.

"Where did you go today, Lara?" he asked the moment she walked in.

She froze, her bag still in her hand. "Nowhere."

"You didn't come to meet me from work. I'd asked you to come this morning."

Her stomach dropped. "I'm sorry, Tristan. I forgot."

In all her turmoil over thinking he might have done something to Mrs Winthorpe, it had completely slipped her mind. Stupid of her. So stupid. Tristan often asked her to meet him from work. How could she have forgotten?

"You stole something from me."

"No, I didn't!" she declared in dismay.

"Yes, you did. You stole a moment from me, a possible opportunity."

"I'm sorry. I didn't mean to."

His fingers curled into fists on his lap. "You know what that means. You need to make it up to me."

"Please, Tristan. I'm tired."

"You're my muse, Lara. You don't get to just suddenly decide that you're not."

"I never said that."

Anyone who came into this house—not that they ever had any guests—would have first had their attention caught by the many portraits hung on the walls. Their presence embarrassed Lara, but there was no way Tristan would ever take them down. He was proud of the paintings. The style was in the form of eighteenth-century oil paintings, with a modern twist.

It wasn't that he was a bad painter, quite the opposite. He had a talent that couldn't be denied. The peachy tone of her skin, to the gentle swell of her breast and the dusky pink of her nipple. She always positioned herself to hide her mound of pubic hair, an arm across her lap or her legs folded, but she couldn't protect her modesty completely. And he always managed to capture every little detail on her body, even the imperfections—especially the imperfections, Tristan would say—the stretch marks and the dimples. The additional roll of fat that had appeared around her middle over recent years, despite her attempt to eat well. He said they made the paintings more beautiful, that people would be able to relate to them more than perfection. She couldn't point out to him that no one else ever saw the artwork. Tristan talked constantly about when the time came for him, he'd have his own show and galleries would be fighting over themselves to display his work. Lara believed his work was good—better than good—but to do well in this area, you needed to be exceptional.

Of course, she'd never say as much to Tristan. She would never risk the wrath of his reaction. He lived for his art. A part of her was jealous that he had something he was so passionate about. What did she have in her life? Him, and her job. That was all. There was nothing she believed in with that much enthusiasm. For as long as she could remember, it had all been about Tristan. He'd been her sun, until she'd found herself completely eclipsed by him, a mere shadow.

"Take off your clothes, Lara."

"Can't we do this one with me dressed?" she pleaded. "Or if not dressed, maybe with a scarf or something."

"I want you naked," he insisted. "It's part of my brand."

"It just feels weird. I wish you could understand that."

"You're like an inanimate object to me when I'm painting," he said. "I certainly don't think of you in any way that should make you feel as though you should cover up to protect yourself. Honestly, Lara, it disturbs me that you would let that thought cross your mind."

He did seem truly disgusted at her, and shame bloomed deep inside her, making her want to shrink into nothing. Was it her? Was there something wrong with her to make her think that way?

"It was a stupid thing to say," she reluctantly agreed. "I just thought an addition of a scarf, maybe draped across my hips or something, would give you a new focus. You could work with the different colours and textures."

His eyes darkened. "Are you trying to tell me how to do my work? Who's the artist here, me or you?"

"I'm sorry, Tristan. I didn't mean anything by it."

"You're a cleaner," he growled. "Stick to what you know best."

I'm also your model, she thought but couldn't bring herself to say. *Where would your art be if you didn't have me?*

Instead, she ducked her head. "Forget I said anything."

He turned away from her. "I already have."

Why couldn't she just say no to him? Yes, she was frightened of him, but his hold on her wasn't physical. He hadn't punched her or kicked her, or pushed her down, instead he withdrew from her, punishing her with stony silences that went on for days. She wanted to leave, but she didn't know how to survive without him, but emotionally and physically, she was adrift. Tristan had accused her of stashing money away, and she knew why he would think that. If she had a little pot of money of her own, it would give her options. As things were, she was broke and had no idea where to start. She didn't know how it felt to live alone, to choose her own surroundings, to decide what she wanted to eat every night without having to take into account what someone else might like. She didn't know how to live where she didn't have someone else to report to.

There were people who helped women escape situations like hers, but she felt like a fraud by even thinking about seeking such help. Tristan didn't hit her, or starve her, or anything like that. He painted her. People would say that he worshipped her. What on earth did she have to complain about? But he made her deeply uncomfortable in a way she couldn't voice. And he controlled her. He was aware of every single thing she did. He made sure he took her last penny off her, asking for receipts for anything she bought. Deep down, she knew it wasn't right, but who would she be in this world without him by her side? She didn't know who she was without him.

Taking a breath and keeping her head down so she didn't need to meet his eye, she unbuttoned the front of her shirt and dropped it to the floor. Then her hands went to her jeans, and she popped the button and yanked down the zipper, before wriggling them from her hips and stepping out of their puddle. She held back a sob as she reached behind her back and undid the clasp of her bra, and let it fall, and finally rolled down her knickers.

Naked, she moved to the chaise longue in the conservatory and got into position, lying on her side, one hand propped beneath her head.

"Relax, Lara," Tristan grumbled from behind the easel. "You know I can't paint you when you're stiff as a board."

She blew out a breath and forced her shoulders to drop and her jaw to relax. She needed to take herself somewhere else, allow her thoughts to drift and her imagination to wander. She dreamed of running away to a place she could be alone, maybe to a small cottage with a courtyard, perhaps near the sea. She would walk on the beach in the early morning and return to the cottage to have a late breakfast of croissants and a sweet latte.

Sitting for Tristan took hours at a time and was hard work. He didn't seem to care about her discomfort. If she grew cold or stiff, he would huff out his annoyance in heavy breaths rather than voicing his displeasure.

She was like an object to him. A thing. Sometimes, she wondered, did he even consider her to be human?

Chapter Twenty-Three

"Aaran Dunsted definitely isn't the killer."

Erica looked up from her computer to where DC Rudd stood beside her desk.

"We know this for sure?" she asked.

Though there had been a third attack on a woman who fit the profile while Dunsted's whereabout had been known, there was always the possibility that one perpetrator had copied another.

"I did some digging. Turns out, Dunsted is the brother-in-law of PC Jeff Perks, who also happens to be one of the attending officers who initially responded to Ian Wilcox's emergency call."

Erica sat up straighter in her chair. "You mean his brother-in-law was one of the first people who would have seen Emma Wilcox's body?"

"Exactly. And there's a chance he told his wife all about it, and though he possibly swore his wife to secrecy, she let it slip to her brother."

She let out a frustrated sigh. "What a fucking waste of time. Bring PC Perks in and grill him about what he might or might not have said to his wife. I want to know for sure that he told her. In fact, bring the wife in, too."

"Yes, boss."

"And get Aaran Dunsted back in here. I want to talk to him."

Rudd nodded and then turned and left.

Erica put her elbows on her desk and her head in her hands. She was annoyed at herself for falling for Aaran Dunsted's bullshit.

Shawn arrived at his desk. "Everything okay?"

"Yeah, just got confirmation that Dunsted definitely isn't our killer."

"That's a good thing, isn't it?" Shawn said. "It means whoever attacked Victoria Greg is more likely to be the same person who killed Emma Wilcox and Kerry Norris."

She wished she could share his positive attitude, but they still didn't know who was attacking these women, and with the third victim still unconscious, she felt like time was running out.

"How did we get on with the other neighbours?" she asked. "Did any of them see anything?"

He shook his head. "Not until after she'd first been spotted. Most of them woke up at the neighbour directly opposite shouting for an ambulance to be called, though some didn't wake until the ambulance and police sirens got them out of bed. Unfortunately, no one's been able to tell us anything useful."

"What about the neighbours who back onto the property? He broke in through the window at the rear, so he may have got out that way, too."

"There are uniformed officers going door-to-door around the surrounding area as well. I'll let you know if they come across anyone who might have noticed anything unusual."

"I'm thinking he might have disturbed something else—maybe broken a fence or set a dog off barking. It might give us an idea which direction he went in, and how he's travelling to and from the houses he's decided to break into. I want all CCTV from around that area, any sign of cars on the move. I know this is London, but there can't be many on the roads at three a.m. Any home security footage is important, too. We might just have caught that bastard while he was running away. If he panicked, he would have let his guard down."

Erica was determined they'd get the son of a bitch this time. There was no way she was going to let him kill or hurt another woman. Not on her watch. It was bad enough that they had two dead bodies on their hands, and that Victoria Greg was going to be in months of rehab before she could even think about going back to a normal kind of life—if such a thing was possible after what she'd been through. Erica refused to let him get his hands on another innocent woman.

Her thoughts went to how he was choosing his victims.

"What about where Victoria Greg works? Tell me she works in an office on the South Bank?"

He shook his head. "Not exclusively, but she's an estate agent and has property showings there, so she frequents the area regularly."

"How is he choosing his victims?" she mused. "If he's seeing them near where they work, how does he then also know they live on their own? These women aren't attacked by accident. He studies them before he makes his move."

"He could look it up," Shawn suggested. "What about through the council, see who qualifies for a reduction of council tax because they live alone."

"That's definitely worth checking out. If Emma Wilcox had told someone at the council that her husband had left, it might be where he's getting his information from."

"I'll get onto it," Shawn said.

"If it wasn't through the council, how else might he know that she'd separated from her husband so recently?" Erica pressed her fingers to her lips, her mind racing. "Did he overhear her? Maybe she told someone, confided in a friend, perhaps?"

"Over coffee or wine?"

She pointed a finger at Shawn. "Good thinking. Where did these women like to hang out? Did they go for drinks at the same place after work? Or somewhere for lunch? Let's get a subpoena for their credit card and bank statements, see if there's anywhere that comes up on each of their statements."

There had to be something linking them, and she was determined to find it.

• • • •

AARAN DUNSTED WAS BACK in the interview room.

Erica needed to manage her anger and frustration. She wanted to hear that he'd made the whole thing up from his own lips, and she wasn't going to get a confession from him by shouting. She needed to be smart about it.

"Hello again, Aaran," she said, slipping back into the interview room and taking a seat opposite him. "Thank you for coming in. I'm sure you've heard that there's been a third victim."

He folded his arms across his chest. "That's a copycat. It wasn't me."

"We know it wasn't you because we had uniformed police sitting outside your flat all night, and you didn't leave."

"Like I said, it was a copycat."

"Aaran, what would happen if we took you to the first victim's house? Would you be able to show us the position you left her body in? I'll give you a hint, it was different to the first."

PC Perks had only attended the second crime scene. If Dunsted only had whatever information Perks or his sister had given him, he wouldn't be able to tell them anything about the first crime scene outside of what had been reported in the news.

He shrugged. "That was a little while ago now. The details are blurry. I always remember the most recent one the clearest."

Cold satisfaction settled inside her. Of course, it was a blow that the killer was still out there, hurting people, but at the same time she wasn't about to put someone behind bars who didn't deserve to be there. Aaran Dunsted clearly had some psychological issues that needed to be dealt with, and at least now she was able to turn her focus back to finding the real killer.

"Aaran, we know what really happened. You weren't the one who killed those women, were you?"

His eyes widened, and he balled his hands into fists on the table. "I was. I told you I was! I proved it to you."

"We know that your sister is married to one of the attending officers. That's why you were able to describe the scene to us."

Erica wondered if PC Perks's wife had any idea of her brother's mental state. She assumed that she had no idea—or why else would either one of them have told him details about a crime scene? If they thought it was something he'd get off on, they'd surely have kept their mouths shut? Erica remembered how Aaran had first come across when she'd stepped into the interview room with him, how calm and sure of himself he'd been. He hadn't broken into a sweat or allowed his hand to tremble. He'd maintained the perfect amount of eye contact and he'd seemed educated and well spoken. Was that the mask he wore for the rest of the world, too? It was terrifying that someone could walk around acting so completely normal when the person they were hiding beneath believed himself capable of murder.

He frowned, his lips pinching. "I don't know what you're talking about."

"There's no point in denying it. It's not something that's a matter of opinion. We were able to look up the relationship connection. Did your sister or her husband talk about the case?"

"Just because they talked about it, doesn't mean I'm lying."

His knee bounced up and down, and for the first time it looked as though he was losing his cool.

"You're right, it doesn't. But since you also are unable to produce any physical evidence on your side, and the only things you can tell us just happen to be the same as those told by PC Perks, we have to assume you are making this story up. We've seen your bedroom and your collection of newspaper clippings, Aaran. Crime is something you have more than a keen interest in. And since you clearly had nothing to do with the third attack either, as you had police watching you the whole time, I think it's time you ended this façade."

"I *did* commit those murders, DI Swift. Even if it didn't happen through my own hands, I saw every moment in my head. I heard their screams, and I felt their pulses slow and finally stop beneath my fingers. There is more than one way to experience things in this life, and just because I wasn't physically there, doesn't mean I didn't kill them."

Erica tutted and huffed out a breath. "Aaran Dunsted, you're being transferred to a psych ward for evaluation. I hope you understand that wasting police time is a crime and will go on your records, and if there is any point where we believe you deliberately misled us in order to cover up someone else's crime or to open the way for another attack to be committed, you might be charged as an accessory."

She couldn't believe she'd wasted so many resources on this prick. She was tempted to write him up for wasting police time, but it was only a misdemeanour and wasn't worth the paperwork. Besides, he clearly needed psychological help if he thought he'd somehow contributed to those women's murders despite not being there.

She stood and knocked on the door to let the waiting officers know she was done and that they could take him to the psych evaluation.

"You know, you're just my type, DI Swift," Aaran continued as the uniformed police officers carted him away. "Just like those other women were. That's why I was there when it happened. That's why I saw it all."

She'd heard enough. "Get some help, Aaran. You're not well."

"I'm the best I've ever been!"

His voice faded as he was led from the room, the door swinging shut behind him.

Chapter Twenty-Four

S he got back to find Shawn pacing the office.

"About time," he said. "We've had the credit card records come back, and there is one place that's shown up repeatedly on both women's credit cards."

"Tell me."

She took a seat at her desk, and he spread the credit card statements out in front of her, several entries highlighted.

"There's a café attached to a modern art gallery on the South Bank, and both women's cards show they go for lunch there during the week. They also both have annual memberships to the gallery."

"Good job. That must be where he's seeing them. What about Victoria Greg? Does she have a membership?"

"Not that I've been able to find out, but that doesn't mean she doesn't go there. The café is open to the public, so you don't have to actually pay to enter the gallery in order to grab a sandwich or a coffee."

"So, she might have frequented the café without being a member?"

"Exactly. And I have some other good news."

"I like good news." Erica risked a smile.

"A Dr Lundy just called and said that Victoria Greg is awake."

Erica jumped to her feet. "You should have told me already!"

"I wanted to make sure you were aware of the connection with the art gallery café first. I thought it might be something we'd need to ask her."

"Yes, of course. Sorry. We just need to get there in case she takes a turn for the worse again."

He stood and grabbed the keys. "Let's go."

She let Shawn drive and got on the phone to fill DI Carlton in on developments.

"While you're at the hospital," Carlton said, "I'll get down to the gallery and show the photographs of the two victims around to the staff, see if anyone recognises them, or if someone has any kind of reaction to the pictures that seems off."

"I assume if they have memberships. The gallery will have some kind of tracking as to when they were in as well. Maybe they got discounts on their food and drinks, and the entrance times were recorded. We're going to need all that information, plus any CCTV they have. We might be able to catch them on camera, see who they were with or if there was anyone of interest hanging around."

"No problem," he said. "I'll be sure to get all of that. I'll interview anyone who might remember the two women as well."

"And ask them about Victoria Greg, too. If this place is really what's connecting them, then they might remember her as well."

"Anything for you, Swift," he said.

She could hear the smile in his voice.

"Good to hear it." She ended the call and turned to Shawn. "Carlton is going down to the gallery now, seeing what he can dig up."

Shawn nodded. "Good. Though we might not need to worry about it if it turns out Miss Greg remembers who did this to her."

"Let's hope it'll be that easy. Somehow, I doubt it."

At best, they might get a description from the third victim, though experience told her that people who'd been through what she had often had a fractured, if not completely blank memory of events. The mind shut down when it needed to protect itself from memories that might be too traumatising to handle.

Erica wanted to get down to the gallery herself after she'd spoken with Victoria Greg, especially if she said that was a place she went on a regular basis. If she didn't, that didn't completely rule out the connection, however. Victoria Greg worked nearby, just as the other women had—within walking distance, anyway—and so she might have been seen simply passing.

"What are you thinking?" Shawn asked, glancing over at her. "You think it might be another customer or someone who works at the gallery, even?"

"Possibly. It's the only connection we can find between the women, other than them all working on the South Bank. There might be other bars and restaurants that all three of them go to as well."

"But on a regular enough basis to need a membership?" He cocked an eyebrow.

"Yeah, maybe not."

She chewed at a hangnail on her thumb, realised she was making it worse, and yanked her hand from her mouth. She was anxious to speak with Victoria Greg as well. What if they got there and she was unconscious again? Time felt as though it was slipping away. The killer had screwed up with Victoria and hadn't been able to get his hit of death. Did that mean he already had his eye on someone new, or had he been scared off and he was hiding away and keeping his head down? She dreaded getting that call saying there had been another murder. Each day that passed where they hadn't put the killer behind bars was another day closer to a potential innocent woman dying. If that happened, she couldn't help but feel responsible.

"What do you think of Carlton?" she asked Shawn.

He shrugged one shoulder. "He's all right."

"Doesn't seem a bit pushy?"

He didn't glance over at her this time but instead kept his eyes firmly on the road. His fingers tightened around the steering wheel. "No more than most other detectives."

She changed the subject. "Dad's back at the care home now. Did I tell you?"

His fingers loosened on the wheel. "No, you didn't. That's good news."

"Yeah, it's a relief. I hate it when he's not well, especially when I need to work on a case. I feel guilty thinking about him when I should be focusing on catching the killer, and then I feel guilty *not* thinking about him because I'm focusing on trying to catch a killer."

"Yeah, and you have Poppy," he pointed out. "No wonder you feel pulled in every direction."

She let out a sigh. "Yes, poor Poppy. I worry she gets forgotten with everything else."

"You're a good mum. She loves you. Look what an inspiration you must be to her. She'll know she can do anything because she's grown up watching her mum do it."

She threw him a grateful smile. "Or she'll grow up resenting me for never being around." *And hate me because my job got her dad killed.*

"Nah, it's a kid's job to resent their parents for something." Erica laughed.

They pulled into the hospital car park and climbed out.

Erica glanced up at the building. "Fucking place."

Shawn shot her a look of amusement. "Not a fan?"

"You know I'm not. I can handle broken arms and lacerated faces, people who've stuck something somewhere they shouldn't, but I can't handle actual sick people. Germs are everywhere."

"You're in the wrong job, Swift. Some of the shit we have to deal with..."

"That's different."

He laughed. "No, it isn't."

"If I'd decided to become a doctor, *then* you could tell me I was in the wrong job."

He chuckled. "I would, too."

"I know you would."

They entered the hospital, and Erica led the way to the Intensive Care unit where she'd previously visited the victim.

She introduced herself to the nurse behind the reception desk.

"Ah, yes, we've been expecting you. Let me buzz Dr Lundy and let him know you're here."

"Thanks."

They took a seat, but no sooner had her backside hit the plastic, the dark head of Dr Lundy came around the corner.

He spotted her and smiled. "DI Swift. Thanks for coming in so quickly."

"It's important. This is my sergeant, DS Turner."

"We spoke on the phone, I believe," Lundy said, and the two men nodded at one another. "Like I told you earlier, Miss Greg is still in an extremely fragile state. I'd prefer if you didn't stay much longer than ten minutes, less if she appears to be struggling. I don't want her heart rate increased because she's upset or stressed. She still has a tube inserted into her lung because of the piercing from her broken rib."

Erica nodded. "Of course."

A different police officer had been sitting with the victim, and, upon hearing their voices outside the door, Erica assumed, he stepped out to give them a quick progress report.

When they were done, the doctor gestured for them to enter the room.

The woman in the bed did not look in a good way. Tubes ran into the veins on the backs of her hands, attached to a pump offering a mixture of fluids and medication. It was impossible to tell which of her injuries occurred during the fight with the man who'd broken into her house to kill her, and which had happened when she fell, but she was a mess. Her lips were swollen and split, and the skin around her eyes bulged like the blood beneath was trying to escape. Grazes streaked across her cheeks and forehead. Though it was hard to see because of the hospital gown, Erica knew there were marks on the woman's skin that definitely couldn't be attributed to the fall from her first-storey window. The red marks and dark bruises around her throat could only ever have been caused by another person's hands.

Victoria Greg noticed the detectives entering the room and struggled to sit up slightly. She grimaced in pain and gave up.

"It's okay," Erica said, stepping to her bedside. "You don't need to sit up."

Victoria removed the oxygen mask from her face. "Sorry. I hate feeling so useless."

The poor woman appeared utterly drained, as though it took every tiny bit of her strength just to form a word and force it from between her lips.

"My name is DI Swift, and this is DS Turner. We wanted to ask you a few questions, if that's all right?"

"Yes, that's fine." As she spoke, she became breathless and had to take extra sips from the oxygen mask before she continued. "The doctors told me what happened to me, or at least a part of it. Someone broke into my house?" She looked between the detectives as though searching for confirmation.

Erica nodded. "Yes, there are signs of an intrusion."

"And then I either jumped or was pushed out of my bedroom window?" She put the mask back over her face and inhaled.

"We believe there might have been a struggle and that was how you were able to escape. What do you remember of what happened?"

"I'm sorry, but like I told the doctors, I can't remember anything. I don't even remember going to bed that night."

Erica smiled gently. "That's okay. You've been through a terrible trauma. It's quite common to block out something so distressing. It's your mind's way of protecting itself. I know this is difficult, but I have to ask if there would be any other reason why you'd have jumped out of the window that night? Have you ever thought of harming yourself?"

The woman's eyes widened in surprise—as much as they could with all the swelling. "No, not at all. I've never felt that way. The only reason I'd have jumped from that window was because I felt I had no other choice."

Erica gave her a reassuring nod. "I just had to rule out that possibility."

"I understand. I just wish I could remember. He's still out there. You think it's the same man who killed those other women, don't you?" She wheezed for breath. "He might do it again, and I could know something that might help you find him."

"We believe it is the same person, yes."

She blinked back tears. "I could be dead now, like those other women."

"You fought back, at least that's what we think must have happened. It gave you the chance to escape. You were very brave."

She shook her head then winced at the movement. "I'm really not, though. I'm not brave at all. And if I pretend like I did something special and that's the reason I'm still alive, it's like saying those two other women weren't brave enough, or weren't special enough, and that's why they died when I didn't." A tear slipped down her cheek, and she sniffed.

"Not at all. You can still be brave without that taking anything away from the other victims."

"I just don't know why I survived when they didn't."

"It's perfectly normal to feel that way." Erica had asked herself the same thing a thousand times before about Chris. Why him? Why had Nicholas Bailey killed her husband, but somehow she had survived? Chris would never have had someone like Nicholas coming into his life if it wasn't for her. She'd never forgive herself for that.

Victoria's eyes suddenly brightened. "The baseball bat!"

Erica frowned. "What baseball bat?"

"The one I keep beside my bed. Maybe that's the reason I escaped."

Erica turned to Shawn for confirmation, though she was already fairly sure of the answer.

He frowned and shook his head. "We didn't find a baseball bat in your room."

She slumped back against the pillows. "Oh, right. Maybe I was mistaken. I could have moved it and I just don't remember."

"Is that something you'd have done?" Erica asked.

"Well... I don't know why I would have. I always keep it beside my bed."

"Do you keep it there as a weapon?"

"I mean, not in seriousness. I bought it as a bit of a joke, you know, but then I'm a woman living alone."

She trailed off as she must have realised she didn't need to give an explanation. She'd been right to think she might need to have something beside her at night to use as protection.

From the number of casts she was currently in, it had most likely saved her life.

"Perhaps the suspect took it with him," Erica suggested. "Could you have hit him with it? Maybe that was how you bought yourself time to escape."

"Maybe." She looked between the two detectives. "I wish I could remember."

So, the suspect had taken the victim's baseball bat with him, but why? Had he realised it would have had his DNA on it? Maybe he took off his gloves and his prints were on the wood? Or perhaps he'd simply thought that he might have needed protection.

If he'd pushed her from the window rather than grabbed her and dragged her back inside, what had he been thinking? Had he known that he'd been out of time? Her opening the window and shouting for help had thrown him. He'd panicked and hit her, hoping she would die in the fall, rather than let her jump and control her own fall, so making it more likely she would survive and be able to go on to tell the police what she'd seen and heard.

"Miss Greg, did you ever go to the modern art studio on the South Bank? Perhaps for coffee or during a lunch break?"

She frowned. "Well, yes. I'm not much one for art, but they have a really good café."

Erica exchanged a hopeful glance with Shawn. They were finally onto something. She was certain the art gallery, or possibly simply the café, was how he was choosing the women.

"Can you remember the last time you were in there?"

Her gaze darted towards the window as she thought, but then she shook her head, a huff of air puffing from her nostrils in frustration. "I'm really sorry, but I honestly have no idea. When I think back, I can't seem to separate any of the days out."

"That's okay. You're doing your best. What about when you did go—were you more likely to use cash or a card?"

"I know it's not fashionable, but I've always preferred to pay for things in cash. It's always seemed more real to me, you know? Like everyone swipes everything onto a card, and they don't really feel like they're spending money." She had to stop and pause for breath, the strangled sound of her wheezing painful to hear.

This was all clearly taking it out of her.

Doctor Lundy stepped in. "I think that's enough for now. We need to let our patient rest."

Erica smiled at him. "Of course." She turned to the woman in the bed. "Thank you for your time. We might need to come back and ask you some more questions, but for the moment, we'll leave you to get better."

Victoria nodded and picked up the oxygen mask again and slipped it over her face. She sank deeper into the bed, and her eyes drifted shut.

Erica clenched her fists in anger. How could someone do this to a vibrant young woman with everything going for her? She was determined to find the son of a bitch and make sure he never hurt anyone else.

• • • •

AS THEY LEFT THE HOSPITAL, her phone rang.

"Swift," she answered.

"It's Carlton. I wondered how you'd got on with Victoria Greg."

She mouthed 'Carlton' to Shawn and then focused on the call. "Her memory of her attacker is non-existent, but she confirmed that she does frequent the gallery, or at least the café there."

"Good. So, we're definitely onto something by focusing in on the place."

"There's something else, too."

"I'm listening."

"She says there was a baseball bat down the side of her bed, that she'd bought it as a bit of a joke but ended up keeping it there for protection. But I don't remember a baseball bat being found at the scene, do you?"

He paused down the line, and she could almost hear the shake of his head.

"No, I don't. You think her attacker might have taken it?"

"She said she kept it there in case of this exact sort of thing happening, and she managed to get away. I think she might have hit him with it, and that was enough for her to make her escape."

She glanced over at Shawn to see if he was following along. He nodded to show he was and that he agreed with everything she was saying.

"And then he took it," Carlton said.

"He's been careful not to leave any traces of DNA at each of the crime scenes so far, but if she was able to hit him with the bat, his DNA would have been all over it. We need to do a search for a baseball bat around the property and nearby streets. There's a chance he may have dumped it somewhere."

For the first time, she experienced a spark of excitement that they might finally have something they could go on. They needed to find that bat, though.

"He's careful, but that carefulness might work against him. He might have thought it would be too dangerous to keep the bat with him, that if he'd been stopped while it was in his possession, it would have raised some questions. And if Victoria had remained conscious after she'd fallen from the window, and had been able to answer questions right away at the scene, the bat would have been one of the first things she would have mentioned. He might have thought he couldn't risk having it on him so would have dumped it at the first possible opportunity."

"I'll contact POLSA," Carlton said, referring to the Police Search Advisory. "We'll want as many officers as we can get on this. We'll search every inch, every dustbin, behind every fence anywhere that he might have thrown it."

"Are we assuming he was on foot then?" she said.

"For a certain distance, yes. No one reported hearing or seeing a car start up on Victoria's street. He wouldn't have risked it. Besides, we recorded the licence plates of all the cars on the street right after the attack. If any were out of place, we'd have followed it up."

Erica tapped her fingers to her lips. "If he was already in the vehicle and gone before the responding officers turned up, that won't have helped us much."

"Do you think he got rid of the bat before he reached the car?"

"Would you have wanted that bat in a car with you if you'd just attacked someone and they'd escaped?"

"No, I guess not."

"You'd get rid of it, and as soon as possible," Carlton said. "We just have to figure out where."

Chapter Twenty-Five

They got POLSA on board and pulled in as many officers as possible to search the streets around Victoria Greg's home.

They divided up into pairs, each walking slowly down both sides of the street, while another group took the road behind the property, checking back gardens and narrow lanes. They opened wheelie bins and hauled out the contents, and beat down long grass, and checked beneath bushes.

Some of the residents weren't happy about the invasion, but they were covered under the PACE act, so there wasn't much they could do about the swarm of police officers crawling over their gardens. Some were probably more worried about their own misdemeanours, paranoid that the bit of weed they smoked on the odd occasion might be discovered, but once they'd been informed of the reasons, the majority were more than happy to cooperate. They'd all heard of the attack and the link with the two other women who'd been murdered, and most were horrified that something like that had gone on close to home. It was easy to feel as though something terrible that happened to someone else had little chance of affecting you, when it was so distanced, but when it was literally on your doorstep, it became very real. Maybe the men didn't care as much as the women, but no one wanted a killer to break into their homes in the middle of the night. The silent, careful way he did it, without disturbing any neighbours—until now—also frightened the residents. The idea of waking up with a stranger standing over your bed was a thing of nightmares.

Come on, come on, come on.

Erica braced herself for a shout of triumph, willing someone to find what they were looking for. They needed this breakthrough. Erica was certain he'd be ramping himself up for another attack. Yes, he might have been spooked by Victoria getting away, but it would also have left him frustrated. He hadn't got his fix. Whatever desire he sated through killing those women and then arranging them in the way he did still remained, and he was probably finding it harder and harder to function with the need still clawing away inside him.

But the minutes and then hours passed, and they still hadn't found what they were looking for.

"Shit," Erica spat out the curse. "Shit, fucking shit. He's going to kill again. I know it. We're not moving fast enough on this. He's got a taste for it now. I bet he's already got his eye on whoever he plans on attacking next, and if we don't figure this out, we're going to be too late."

"Victoria Greg escaping might have spooked him," Shawn said. "He might think it's too dangerous to try again."

"It'll be killing him if he's trying to hold off."

Eventually, they had to admit they weren't going to find anything, and the search was called off.

Erica couldn't shake the funk she found herself in at them not locating the bat. She'd been so certain it would be the solid lead they needed.

They still had the gallery coffee shop, she told herself, trying not to be as disheartened as she felt. They hadn't reached a dead end just yet.

Carlton had been to the gallery and shown the women's photographs around, but he'd told her that while a couple of the girls serving behind the counter had recognised the women, no one had caught his eye as being suspicious. They'd requested entrance records to find out when the first two victims had used their membership cards to enter the gallery, and they had a couple of officers going through the CCTV footage from the gallery and café. He'd interviewed a number of people who worked there, but no one had highlighted themselves as being persons of interest, and background checks on them hadn't revealed anything worse than a couple of speeding tickets.

Erica needed to go there herself. She had to get a feel for the place, watch the faces of the people who worked there, study the clientele. She decided to take the rest of the day to go and spend some time there, just as a customer, not as a detective. If she needed to reveal her real reason for being there then she would, but for the moment she didn't want to draw any additional attention to herself. Her instincts told her that the killer would be planning another attack soon, and if he hadn't already picked his next victim, he could well be on the lookout.

• • • •

SHE STOOD ON THE STREET outside the gallery and assessed the buildings nearby, the ones adjacent to the gallery and across from it, making a note of which ones had security cameras outside.

The gallery was far larger than she'd imagined, even after she'd checked the place out online. She'd never been particularly interested in art, but especially not modern art, where, in her opinion, it all looked a bit like children had been colouring in shapes, or did things like throw a fake bedroom together and call it art. Not that she had any artistic talent herself. She could barely manage to draw a stick person.

Erica took the steps up to the entrance and pushed through the glass doors into a large foyer. Directly ahead was an entrance desk with a smartly dressed, very thin woman standing behind it. Over to her right was the entrance to the café, and to her left were the signs for the toilets.

She approached the desk. "Entry for one, please."

The thin woman raised a bright smile. "Can I interest you in one of our membership cards?"

"Not for the moment, thank you."

"How about one of our guides? It gives you a little more background on each painting than what's on the wall and tells you where each part of the exhibition is located."

That actually did sound helpful, so she accepted and paid for both the guide and the ticket. She'd go and sit in the café and nurse a coffee once she'd been around the exhibition. Maybe then she'd reveal who she was, together with her real reasons for being here.

Erica thanked the woman for her ticket and picked up the guide. The ticket had a barcode that she beeped against a metal turnstile, as though she was at a train station instead of an art gallery, and she followed the wide corridor down to the main exhibition room.

She wasn't alone in the building either. Other visitors wandered past her, and she found herself checking each of their faces, wondering if they might be the killer.

She passed a security guard in a uniform, who nodded a greeting to her.

Could it be him? He'd see plenty of people coming and going, including both of the first victims, since they were regular visitors. Maybe he'd seen Victoria Greg in the café during his lunch break? She wondered how many other guards worked here and made a mental note to see if Carlton had asked for a full staff list when he'd been here.

Stepping out of the corridors, she found herself in a vast open space. The walls were all white, with equally white rectangular pillars breaking up the room. A shiny, polished concrete floor was beneath foot. Though this was a gallery for displaying art, she was surprised at the lack of paintings on the walls. They seemed sparse, in simple frames, hung with massive spaces between each piece. Some of the paintings were several feet tall, while other were mere inches.

People walked around, speaking quietly, heads together, some using the same guide she'd bought at the desk to educate themselves about the artwork. It was a mixture of suits and young fashionistas. Bearded men and women in jeans with more leg showing than denim.

She glanced down at the pamphlet in her hand, aware she hadn't opened it. The truth was that she was more interested in the people than she was the art.

Looking around, she realised she'd been a little harsh in her opinion, and actually modern wasn't really that modern at all. Some of this work went back to the eighteen hundreds. Did that make it any better? Maybe it did. At least with the older work they actually used paints rather than random bits of metal and brick.

Erica made her way around the space and then took an exit on her right. She entered another room of art installations. A wall, with graffiti on it. A black metal structure in the shape of a torso. A pile of skulls with wooden poles poking out of the empty eyeballs. A couple of people—a man and a woman, both in dark suits—appeared to be installing another piece. Were they the creators of the artwork or simply the people putting it together? If they worked here, they, too, would be in a position to see people coming or going.

For a moment, the possibility of the killer being one of the artists entered her head, but she dismissed it. How much were the artists even involved here once their work was on display?

She sensed eyes on her and glanced over her shoulder.

The man who'd been putting one of the installations together was staring at her. He caught her eye, and the corners of his lips curled in a smile, and he ducked his head in a nod.

Her gaze flicked to the front of his jacket, hunting for a name tag that would tell her who he was, but he wasn't wearing one. She could easily take her own ID from her pocket and demand for him to tell her, but she didn't want to give away her identity or her reason for being here. She wanted to appear like a normal customer.

Erica returned the smile and turned away. When she got back to the office, she'd get the staffing list from Carlton and do some searches on the names. Whoever had spotted both Emma Wilcox and Kerry Norris had been at the gallery and might have noticed them just like this man was noticing her now.

An idea was forming in her mind.

She moved slowly through the rest of the gallery, leafing through her guide as she went, stopping in front of various portraits and pretending to be interested in them while watching the people around her.

Finally, she emerged back where she'd started, and she realised she'd done the whole gallery. The only place she hadn't been yet was the café.

It was lunchtime, and, as she'd expected, the place was busy. The clink of cups and plates and the hum of conversation filled the air. It was clear that not all of these people were here for the art. Young professionals made up the majority of the visitors, but there was also families and a handful of students, too.

Erica joined the queue at the counter. A couple of women were serving, bustling around to plate up sandwiches and cakes and frothing milk from a hissing steamer. They were efficient, and within minutes Erica was being served. She ordered an Americano and a chicken and pesto focaccia sandwich. She had to admit that it did look good. She understood why everyone was so keen on coming here.

Her order was handed to her, and she glanced around for a spare table. A young man in a suit saw her hunting for one and rose from his table, gesturing to her that he was leaving.

"Thanks," she told him as he left.

Could he be the killer? Everyone was a possible suspect. The seat she was in gave her a view over the counter and much of the café—a perfect people-watching position.

She added two packets of sugar into the coffee and debated shaking some of the Tabasco sauce in her bag onto the sandwich.

Wanting to blend in with everyone else, she got out her phone and pretended to scroll through it, while surreptitiously observing everyone else. Was the man she'd caught the eye of inside the gallery in here? Did there seem to be anyone else who was spying on other people, perhaps hunting for their next victim?

Erica dragged out the coffee and sandwich for as long as she could. No one acted suspiciously or caught her attention. She fought against the desire to question everyone, to show photos of the murdered women and demand to know if anyone recognised them and if they'd ever seen them with a man who might either work here, or else be another regular, but she wanted to keep hold of her anonymity.

She stood from her chair.

"Shit!"

Her elbow collided with someone walking past her.

"Watch it!"

A puddle of milky coffee covered the floor.

Erica turned her attention to the person she'd collided with.

The other woman was in her twenties, Erica guessed, with straight, dark-brown hair and wide blue eyes. Her jeans were too baggy for her slender frame, and her oversized jumper now had a splash of brown down the front.

"Oh my God, I'm so sorry. I wasn't paying attention."

A flash of dismay distorted her pretty features as she stared down at the mess, but the expression was quickly covered with a smile. "Oh, don't worry. It was only an accident."

Erica scooped up some clean serviettes from the table and handed them to the woman to dab herself down with. "Let me buy you another coffee, at least. Or pay for your dry cleaning."

"No, there's no need for all that. It was just an accident, and I know someone who works here, so I can get a replacement coffee. Honestly, it's fine."

She glanced around the café, craning her neck, clearly looking for the person she knew.

"Oh, there he is," she said, lifting her hand in a half wave.

Erica spotted an attractive, dark-haired man with a tall, lean physique emerging from the rear of the café, through a door that was marked 'staff only'.

The woman gestured at her jumper. "Don't worry about this. Have a good day."

And then she was gone, weaving her way between the tables towards the man. They greeted each other, and the man frowned at the mess on her top, and she gestured back to where Erica still stood.

The woman had a similar colouring to the man she was meeting. At least that meant she would be safe, Erica realised. Their suspect hadn't chosen any brunettes as victims yet, though there was always a first time. Also, from the kiss the man placed on her cheek, Erica assumed she didn't live alone, though that was something she couldn't be sure about.

The man glanced over and caught sight of Erica standing there. His eyes hardened for a second, and then he turned away, his hand on the woman's lower back as he guided her towards the door.

Chapter Twenty-Six

D uring her time at the art gallery, a plan had formed in Erica's mind.

First, she had to convince Gibbs of it, and it wasn't going to be easy. But without finding the bat so they had DNA that they could use to narrow down any potential suspects, it was the only thing she could think of. Every night that went past without another killing only brought them closer to the night when he *did* kill, and if she didn't try this, there would be blood on her hands, too.

She wanted to get Gibbs on his own. She already knew Turner and probably DI Carlton, too, wouldn't be happy about her idea, but if she had Gibbs behind her, they wouldn't be able to do much to stop her.

Erica stood in front of Gibbs' desk and ran through her plan.

He sat back and folded his arms across his chest. "You're talking about putting yourself up as bait, Swift."

"I'm fully aware of that. We need to lure him out. And like Aaran Dunsted said, I'm just his type. All I need to do is make out like I live alone to get his attention, and I'd fit all his criteria."

"It's dangerous. I don't want one of my detectives putting themselves on a killer's radar like that."

"We put ourselves in dangerous situations every day, and we need to do something. Time is running out, I can feel it. Any day now, we're going to get that call to say he's killed someone else. How are we going to feel if we didn't do everything in our power to find this son of a bitch and put him behind bars?"

He tilted his head to one side, observing her. "You've been through a lot recently, Swift. Should I be worried about you?"

She gave a small laugh. "If you think this is some kind of crazy suicide attempt, I promise you, you're on completely the wrong track, sir. There is nothing wrong with my mental health. I'm just one hundred percent committed to finding this guy."

He sighed and ran a hand over his mouth. "There must be something else we can do."

"If you can think of another plan, I'm all ears."

She knew he didn't have anything.

"Look," she continued, "it might not amount to anything. I'll go and hang out at the gallery, buy a membership, drink coffee, just like I did before, only this time I'll take Rudd with me. We'll be like two girlfriends gossiping, and I'll talk about how hard it is for me now that Chris has gone and I'm living alone."

He compressed his lips to a thin line. "And then what?"

"We make sure my house is covered by police and hope he takes the bait."

"The bait being you?"

"My back door has glass in it," she continued. "I'll leave the key in the lock so he can cut a hole and then reach through and let himself in. I'll be ready for him, and I trust my colleagues will take care of me. Once he attacks, we'll be able to nail the bastard."

"And if he doesn't?"

She shrugged. "Then we're in no worse a position than we currently are, but the amount of time I spend at the gallery café might still help. It's the one thing linking all the victims, and it's the only thing we've got right now."

He let out a slow, considered sigh, and she knew he was thinking about it.

"Okay, fine. We'll do it, but with one main difference. It won't be your house it happens at. The Met own some residential properties. Let me find out which ones are empty, so you can put that down as being your home address."

She nodded in agreement. "As long as the property has the same access profile, that will be fine."

A part of her was relieved at the suggestion. She didn't really like the idea of letting the killer know her address, or the thought of someone breaking into her home. It would mess with her head. Plus, even though she was certain they'd catch him, there was always the possibility that they wouldn't. How would she feel safe with Poppy in their home if they didn't?

"One other thing," he continued, "you need to be covered by someone else the whole time. Don't take any risks."

"Thank you, sir. I won't let you down.

• • • •

"NO." SHAWN SHOOK HIS head, his arms folded. "You're not going to do that."

She raised an eyebrow. "I'm doing it. Gibbs has already signed it off."

"Gibbs is wrong," he muttered. "It's too dangerous."

"I won't be on my own." She was trying to reassure him. "I'll have Rudd with me at the gallery, and you and Carlton can watch the house he's allocated to me. If he comes for me, we'll have him."

"I think it's a good idea," Carlton said, half perched on her desk, his stance relaxed. "You do match the victims' profiles."

Shawn's eyes narrowed. "Don't encourage her. There has to be another way."

"If there is one, tell me," Erica said. "This is police work. We know he's seeing them at the gallery. I'd put money on Emma Wilcox telling a friend over coffee about her marital problems and he overheard."

Her sergeant still wasn't sold on the idea. "There must be another way to figure out who it is. We can narrow it down at least."

"How many people passed through the gallery every day?" she said. "Curators, installers, cleaners, visitors. The list is endless. We can't narrow down that number of people."

He didn't give up. "First of all, we can probably halve that?"

She folded her arms, matching his stance. "How?"

"We think he's most likely male."

Carlton joined in. "He also must be fairly strong and fit. He climbed onto the balcony of the first victim's flat, and the extension roof at the third crime scene. There's no way someone who wasn't in great shape would be able to achieve that."

Shawn nodded, clearly liking his train of thought. "Under forty then or, if he's older, he's extremely physically fit for his age?"

Erica exhaled a frustrated sigh. "Okay, that probably halves it down again, but we're still looking at potentially a hundred or more men. Even if we brought every single one of them in for questioning, there's no certainty we'd know who the killer was. We could just let him walk right out of there again, and then he goes on to murder another woman, laughing at us the entire time."

Shawn shook his head and turned away. "This is crazy."

"It's the right thing to do, Turner. I'll be fine. I'll have all of you there to watch out for me. I trust you with my life."

• • • •

THAT EVENING, SHE WENT to pick up Poppy from Natasha's. There was something she needed to talk to her sister about, and she wasn't looking forward to it.

"Is it okay if you have Poppy overnight tomorrow?" she asked as she stepped into the house.

Her sister picked up Poppy's bag and handed it to her. "You know she's welcome any time."

She was pushing her luck. "Is it okay if it's for a couple of nights? I have a work thing."

Natasha frowned. "A work thing? Are you going away somewhere? A conference or something."

"Yes, something like that, though I'll still be in the city, if there's an emergency."

Her frown deepened, and she angled her head to one side like a curious dog. "You'll be in the city, but you won't be able to see your daughter?"

"No, not until this is done, sorry."

"Erica," she said, a warning tone to her voice. "What's going on?"

"It's a work thing. That's all you need to know."

"A work thing you need to get your daughter out of the way for? Please tell me this isn't something dangerous." Her eyes lit up and then darkened again. "It's to do with this case, isn't it?" She lowered her voice. "About those poor women being murdered."

"I really can't talk about it, Tasha. I'm sorry."

"Please, don't do anything stupid, especially after what happened with Chris."

"I won't, but I have to catch this son of a bitch. He's out there, planning the next one, and we have no idea who he is."

"What about your family, Erica? Isn't it about time you put us first? Does it ever occur to you that you might be putting us in danger, too?"

Erica reached out and took her sister's hand. "I'm doing this for you, and for people like you. If I don't do my job, then people like him will be out on the streets, killing whoever they like. Do you really want your children, as well as Poppy, to grow up in a world like that?"

"No, I'd never want that." Natasha squeezed her fingers. "I just don't understand why it always needs to be you who takes the risks."

"It isn't, Tasha. Every single police officer who gets up in the morning and goes to work is taking a risk for the rest of us. They all have their own lives—children, and sisters, and husbands. All people they're trying to protect. What makes me any different?"

"You've already lost someone important to you. You've already made that sacrifice. *That's* why it should be someone else."

Erica appreciated her sister's concern, but she needed to look at the bigger picture. How could Erica *not* do this? What if another woman died, and Erica hadn't done everything in her power to stop it?

She didn't want to give Natasha the details about what she was doing. The more she knew, the more it might put her in danger, and as her sister had pointed out, just being Erica's family was dangerous.

"Please, will you just have Poppy?"

Natasha let out a long sigh. "Of course I will."

"Thank you."

By the time she picked up her daughter in a couple of days, Erica hoped they'd have the killer safely behind bars.

Chapter Twenty-Seven

Just as they'd planned, Erica and DC Rudd visited the gallery together.

This time, Erica accepted the offer of a membership card and filled in the details, which included the address of the house the Met owned that she'd be staying at, and paid the additional cost. She'd claim it back from expenses. She still had the guide from her previous visit, so Rudd bought a copy instead.

Slowly, they made their way around the gallery. Between discussing the artwork, Erica made sure to chat about how hard life had been since Chris had died. It was difficult for her to talk about him, though a part of her felt as though she was acting. She could tell it wasn't easy for Heather Rudd to listen to her DI discussing such personal matters either. But they both needed to get over their awkwardness in order to appear natural, so they did their best to think of themselves as friends rather than colleagues. Hannah had several flatmates, so she didn't fall into the category of living alone.

They passed a couple of security guards, and Erica made sure to raise her voice slightly.

"I think it's knowing no one else is in the house that makes it harder. No one to warm up the bed at night, if you know what I mean."

"Yeah, it must be difficult to go from being married to being on your own," Rudd agreed.

A lump choked her throat. "It is. It really is. He was a good man, and he didn't deserve what happened to him."

They kept going, doing the rounds, continuing the conversation but varying it slightly each time. When there was no one else around, they dropped into exchanging observations about the people they'd passed or anyone who might have paid them any extra attention. But the moment another visitor or someone else who worked at the gallery grew near, they switched back to Erica being alone in the house.

Once they'd done a couple of rounds of each of the rooms of the gallery, they made their way to the café. Erica kept an eye out for the man the woman she'd spilt coffee on had met, but he wasn't around. She didn't know why he'd caught her attention. She'd looked him up when she'd got back to the office and had managed to pin him down as a Mr Tristan Maher, but there was nothing in his profile that made her think she should be any more suspicious of him than anyone else. Perhaps it was the look he'd given her, but that was probably only because she'd made a mess of the woman's jumper.

They ordered coffee and sandwiches and then took a seat. The last time she'd been here, Erica had hidden herself away in a corner, her back to the wall so she could watch out for everyone else, but this time they found a table right in the middle of the room, with people surrounding them.

They continued the conversation, Erica once more lamenting how hard it was living alone now that Chris was gone. The thing was that she wasn't lying, so though it felt strange speaking about it, she sounded genuine.

Erica turned her head and spotted the woman she'd thrown coffee on the other day pushing her way into the café.

"One minute," she said to Rudd. "I know her."

Rudd nodded and stayed sitting.

Erica rose to her feet and wove between the tables to approach her. Just like before, she appeared to be looking for someone—here to meet the same man she had before. She caught sight of Erica heading towards her.

"Oh, hello again." Erica threw her what she hoped was a warm smile. "You were here the other day, weren't you?"

"Yes, that's right." The woman returned the smile, but it was cautious. "You were the one who spilled coffee down my front."

"Yes, I was. Sorry about that again. Were you able to get the stain out?"

"Yes, it came out. Lucky I drink my coffee milky."

Erica glanced around. "I've only just discovered this place. It's lovely, isn't it? At the risk of sounding like a cliché, is it somewhere you come often?"

She laughed. "Yes, actually, I do. I know someone who works here."

"Of course, you were here to meet your husband?" She let her line of sight drop to the woman's finger but saw no ring. "Sorry, or boyfriend?"

"Oh, no," she said, giving a small laugh. "Tristan's not my husband. He's my brother. My twin brother, actually. I mean, clearly, we're not identical, but we shared a womb and have been together ever since. He's older than me by a few minutes, which is something he's always happy to remind me of."

Erica gave her head a small shake. "Sorry, wrong of me to assume."

"It's fine, honestly. That kind of thing happens a lot. We're very close and obviously we have the same surname. People who don't know us always think we're married."

"And he works here?" Erica enquired. "In the building?" She already knew this but wanted to hear it from the other woman's mouth. She spoke in a way that had a nervous edge to it, fast and always close to an anxious laugh. Was Erica making her nervous, or was it something to do with the brother? She didn't miss the way her gaze kept darting over Erica's shoulder, towards the counter. Was she worried she'd be seen talking to Erica?

"Yes. I mean, he's not one of the curators or anything. He manages the café, but he is actually an artist, and a very good one at that. He hopes to have his work hanging on these walls at some point, but for the moment, I think he's content with just being near to such beauty."

"You sound very proud of him."

"I am, really. He's very talented." She peered anxiously over her shoulder. "I really should get going."

Erica put up both hands. "Don't let me keep you." She paused for a moment and then called out, "What's your name? Just in case I see you again."

"Oh, it's Lara."

"Nice to meet you, Lara. I'm Erica."

She seemed a little unsure as to why Erica was introducing herself, but then her face warmed in a real smile. "Good to meet you."

"You, too."

Chapter Twenty-Eight

When he finished his shift, Lara drove home with Tristan.

"Who was that woman you were talking to?" he asked.

She blinked. "What woman?"

"Pretty. Strawberry-blonde hair. Early thirties. Smartly dressed."

"Oh, the one who bumped into me the other day and tipped my coffee down my front? I don't know her or anything. She said her name is Erica."

"What was she saying to you?"

"Nothing much." Lara shrugged. "Just asking if I came here often, that kind of thing."

He shot her a side glance. "Was she trying to hit on you or something?"

She laughed. "Don't be silly."

He fell silent and then asked, "What are you making for dinner?"

She was relieved at the change in subject. "One of your favourites. Chicken Caesar salad and fresh bread."

"I hope you've made the dressing from scratch. You know how I hate that premade stuff."

"Of course, Tristan."

They arrived at home, and she pulled the car into the drive.

"Good," he said, "because we're celebrating."

She glanced over at him. "We are?"

"I got a phone call today from a smaller gallery over in Brick Lane. They saw my work. They want to give me a showing."

She twisted towards him, her mouth open in shock. "Oh my God, Tristan. That's incredible. Congratulations."

"Thank you. They want to show local artists only for March, and they chose me."

She flung her arms around his neck and hugged him tight. "I'm so proud of you."

She was, too. She'd always been proud of her handsome, talented brother. He was so much more confident and self-assured than her. He knew exactly what he wanted from life and he just went out and took it. She was a mere shadow in comparison to him.

Automatically, she followed him through the house, into his studio.

"What paintings are you planning on showing?" she asked his retreating back.

He looked over his shoulder at her, a frown drawn between his eyebrows, and immediately she realised she'd said something wrong.

"Which ones do you think?"

Her stomach sank. *No, not those!*

Lara lifted her gaze to the wall, at the largest of the framed portraits he'd done of her that hung there. There weren't many times she was happy they had no real social life, and that no one else came to the house, but faced with her portrait in all her naked glory made her grateful no one else would see it. Yet, here he was, implying the exhibition he'd been offered would mean putting the paintings on display, in public—something he'd always promised her would never happen.

"That one is my favourite, Lara." He'd noticed what was focusing her attention. "It will take pride of place in the gallery, and everyone will admire it."

Lara didn't even want to look at the picture, the sight of her own naked body filling her with shame. Was everyone really going to see it? And they'd know that her own brother had painted it, and that she'd lain, naked, in front of him for hour after hour after hour. Would they think she enjoyed it? That she got a perverse kick from her own brother staring at her naked body? Tristan had assured her numerous times before that it wasn't like that at all, and she was simply a form, a figure, and all of his art colleagues would see it the same way, as though she was almost removed from her humanity, but it was far harder for her to see it that way. It had always felt weird to her, wrong, and dirty.

Perhaps she felt this way because he'd always used her sitting for him as a punishment. He'd deliberately made her feel as though she'd done something to displease him and this was a way of her making things up to him.

"But... but I don't want everyone seeing them. I mean," she gestured her hand up and down towards the painting, "I'm naked in them."

"Oh, for goodness' sake, Lara, stop acting like such a child. Paintings are created so that other people can admire and take pleasure from them. Did you really think that no one else would ever see these?"

"I thought you were just practising! I didn't think for one second that they'd end up on a gallery wall."

His gaze darkened. "Just practising? Are you saying that's all these paintings are worthy of... just a bit of practise? An amateur throwing some paint around?"

Her pulse raced. She recognised this part of him, and it never led to anything good.

"No! You know how much I love and admire your work. I've supported you ever since the first day you picked up a paintbrush, and to claim that I am somehow now putting you down is completely unfair. If your paintings were of anyone or anything else, I wouldn't hesitate in saying how wonderful it is that you're finally getting the chance to be hung in a gallery."

"This is a massive opportunity for me, Lara. You have to see that. It's only a small showing, but it could be the start of something really big for me."

Tristan would get his own way, no matter what she said or did. It had been that way their whole lives, ever since they were small children. Whenever she dared to mention something that she might like, it was always guaranteed he'd find some way of taking it off her. Being twins, their birthdays were on the same day and their parents always expected them to share a party. And Tristan always found a way to get what he wanted. If she wanted to go to the zoo one year as their birthday treat, but Tristan wanted to do go-kart racing, he'd beg and promise her that they could do the zoo the following year, and she'd always give in, and then when that following birthday rolled around, he would do the same thing all over again. Even friends they'd had when they'd been kids had always become more Tristan's friends than hers.

She gazed around in horror at all the naked flesh—all of her naked flesh—which he'd managed to replicate in every minute detail in paint. He'd captured every flaw—every roll of fat, every stretch mark, every pimple. She'd believed they would never be seen in public, that he'd simply been perfecting his art by using her as his subject, but now he was claiming that these would be on walls in a professional studio, for people to gawp over.

Her face burned at the thought alone. How would she ever be able to go out in public again? What if someone recognised her? They'd know exactly what she looked like when she was naked, and from all different angles. That they'd all know it was her brother who'd painted her, too, squirmed uncomfortably inside her like a worm in an apple core. He'd seen her in those positions, naked, and had stared at her and studied her, and recreated her in paint. She'd never told anyone that Tristan exclusively painted her.

"You promised me!" she tried again.

"Well, promises change. How about you take a closer look at yourself, Lara. Do you see what you're asking of me? You're basically asking me to give up my one chance at achieving the thing I've worked for all my life because you're what? A little *embarrassed*? Can you hear how ridiculous that sounds? People have already seen the paintings, Lara, and they love them. No one cares about your nudity."

"I care!" she cried. "It's personal."

It *was* personal to her. No one apart from Tristan had ever seen her naked. She was twenty-six years old and she was still a virgin. She'd never even had a boyfriend. Tristan had always seen to that. The moment a man, or when they'd been teenagers, a boy, had started to like her, Tristan would always make sure he scared them away. She never knew exactly what it was he said or did to them, but once Tristan had had his 'word' with them, they never spoke to her again. Sometimes, she'd catch them watching her out of the corners of their eyes with frightened faces, but any possibility of a relationship would be gone.

"If you fuck this up for me, Lara, I swear I'll make you wish you'd never been born. This is the most important thing in my life, and I won't let you ruin it."

"More important than me?"

"Yes. Far more important than you. Who are you anyway, Lara? There's nothing to you. No substance. You've been leaning on me your whole life. Without me, you'll be nothing."

She hated every word he said, while knowing it was true. It hadn't been so bad before their parents had died, but once it was just the two of them, her reliance on him had multiplied tenfold. It had never occurred to her before then that people could simply just stop existing. Of course, she'd always known her parents were older than her and would die one day, but she hadn't been anywhere near prepared to deal with their sudden loss. She'd grown fearful that something would happen to Tristan as well, and then she'd be left alone in the world, and she'd allowed him to take over, becoming even more of his shadow.

Tristan hadn't been affected by their parents' death in the same way she had. The two of them had inherited everything their parents had owned—the house and their savings. Tristan had instantly put a claim on whatever he'd wanted. Their father's car had been a write-off in the accident, so Tristan had insisted he needed to spend at least twenty grand of their inheritance on a decent car for himself, leaving Lara with their mother's little runaround. Not that she'd cared about cars, but when he'd started selling off all their parents' belongings, including her mother's jewellery, she'd been upset. He hadn't even consulted her and instead sold it out from under her nose. When she'd confronted him about it, he'd grown angry and shouted at her, telling her they had bills to pay and no jobs, and that they couldn't eat gold and diamonds.

She'd responded by starting her cleaning company, at first just doing a few hours for the mother of an old school friend who'd taken pity on her, and who then recommended her to another friend and another. When Tristan insisted that she didn't understand the bills that needed to be paid, she handed her money over to him to deal with it all. It was easier that way. There were fewer arguments, and he kept food in the fridge and the light and heating on, and filled up her little car for her. She didn't need her own money—or at least that was what she kept telling herself. When she'd suggested to him that maybe she could start taking some responsibility and take care of her finances, he'd been furious with her, telling her that she clearly didn't trust him and threatening to leave her to get on with things on her own. Now, looking back, she realised she should have taken him up on the offer. She'd had no idea she'd still be in the same situation eight years later.

Lara deflated, suddenly heavy with misery. "You can't blame me for feeling anxious about everyone seeing me naked."

"*You* won't be naked," he said. "You'll be fully clothed, I assure you of that."

"You know what I mean, Tristan."

He stepped closer, then reached out and slipped his hand around the back of her neck, his fingers knotting in her hair.

He lowered his forehead to hers. The gesture might have been meant to be comforting, but instead it felt possessive.

"You're my muse, Lara. You're my inspiration. No one will care if you're dressed or undressed."

"I care!" she cried.

His fingers tightened in the strands of hair, and little darts of hot pain shot through her scalp.

"You should care about me, too," he growled. "I'm your brother. Don't hold me back, Lara. You'll come to regret it."

She held back a whimper. "What's that supposed to mean?"

"You'd never cope without me helping you get through life. You're useless on your own. I've carried you through everything, and now you're complaining about this one tiny little thing you've done for me?"

He released his hold on her hair and turned away from her again, shaking his head. She sensed his disappointment in her radiating off him in waves, and she hated herself for it. Was he right? Was she reading too much into this? It wasn't that she thought she had a particularly bad figure, even by modern standards, but that didn't mean she wanted all Tristan's posh, art-type friends knowing exactly what she looked like naked.

"I'm sorry," she whispered. "I didn't mean to upset you."

"Well, it's too late for that, isn't it, 'cause clearly now I'm upset! And I still have work to do. How am I supposed to get on with what I need to do when you decide to upset me? You know I can't concentrate now."

"Please, Tristan. It's fine. If you really need to show the paintings, then show them."

"Of course I need to show them! What else am I supposed to hang in the gallery? Empty fucking frames?"

What about the paintings you've been working on during the night? What have you done with them?

But she didn't dare say it to him, knowing her question would be met with defensive fury.

"No, Tristan," she said instead, staring at the floor, not daring to meet his eyes in case he saw the question in hers.

"Good. This conversation is over then."

Lara clamped her lips together and clenched her fists by her sides. She wanted to throw herself on the floor and cry and beg that he didn't fill a room with her naked portraits, but it would do no good.

Tristan always got his own way.

• • • •

THE FOLLOWING MORNING, Tristan left for work, leaving Lara alone in the house. He'd been in a good mood at breakfast, chatting about the showing, daydreaming of selling his paintings for large sums of money so he could give up his job in the gallery café and paint full time.

He didn't care that selling the paintings meant he was also selling a part of her, and every word he uttered sank her deeper into depression.

She didn't have any clients on that day, so she decided to spend the day doing their house instead. Cleaning always made her feel better. Not only did it keep her hands and thoughts occupied, she also got satisfaction in transforming a dirty, cluttered room into a place of calm. The thanks and praise she got from her clients once they'd seen her work were often the only nice things anyone ever said to her.

Lara started downstairs, tidying away the breakfast dishes, and then getting to work, decluttering the kitchen counters and wiping down all the surfaces. She was meticulous, never just going around the small white goods, but always moving the toaster and kettle, and microwave, making sure to wipe those items as well as going under and behind them.

The kitchen opened onto the conservatory, which was also Tristan's studio. If she was going to mop the floors, she needed to tidy up in there, too. She'd avoid his work area, his paints and easel—which was currently covered with a sheet anyway—and just go around them.

She wiped down the desk in the corner of the conservatory, and then the bookshelf, and moved onto the radiator cover, lifting the picture frames that contained photographs of them both as children, and then placing them down again.

Something caught her attention, and she frowned, wondering if her eyes were playing tricks on her. Tristan had built the cover over the ugly radiator himself and he'd put the photographs and a scented candle on top. Lara had laughed at the candle and told him it would melt the moment he put the radiator on, but he'd said he didn't like it when it got too hot, anyway. She'd wanted to point out that considering she was the one who was always having to sit still for hours on end with no clothes to keep her warm, that perhaps she might like to have the radiator on. But, of course, she hadn't, and she just got cold instead.

Still, the top of the radiator cover looked different now, though the front was still the same. There appeared to be a line running horizontally across its length, and when she checked down the side, the line continued. It was almost as if the whole front piece came away.

Maybe that was simply how it had been built? That was just where the front panel went on, wasn't it? Except, it didn't seem right, as though it was additional to the front panel.

Curious, Lara hooked her fingernails into the line that ran across the top. She pulled back on it. It lifted.

"Oh!"

She dropped it again, and it slotted back into place, but her curiosity had only intensified.

It wasn't an extra panel. It was a hidden one.

It reminded her of the part of a beehive the beekeeper would slide out to scrape off the honey, or the part under the toaster that collected the crumbs and then could be pulled out to empty. But what was it doing as part of a radiator cover?

This must be Tristan's. He wouldn't want you to go nosing around something he's deliberately hidden.

The voice in her head was right, but how could she not investigate now? It would bug at her constantly, scraping at her nerve endings, chewing at the corners of her mind. She wouldn't be able to look at Tristan without mentally asking him about it. Did it have something to do with the painting he was doing during the night?

Lara glanced over her shoulder, half expecting to find him behind her, but he was at work and she was alone. That knowledge didn't stop her heart racing or her palms growing slick with sweat. Tristan really wouldn't want her poking around his belongings, but this was as much her house as his. Just because he'd claimed the conservatory for his own, didn't mean she was barred from the room. She had every right to be here.

Besides, there was still a part of her that was angry with Tristan because of the exhibition. If they hadn't had that argument, and if he hadn't insisted on going ahead with it, no matter what her views or feelings were on the matter, perhaps she would have respected his privacy a little more. Since Tristan clearly had no respect for her privacy, she didn't see why it should come from her either.

She wiped her hands on her thighs then hooked her nails back down the crack. She jiggled the panel, ascertaining it was definitely loose, and lifted it.

The internal panel slid out. It had a back to it, so created a kind of very shallow drawer, the same height and width as the radiator cover. And it wasn't empty.

Lara recognised the contents of the drawer instantly. The sheets of paper were the same ones Tristan painted on. The thick, slightly rough texture of the treated paper was what Tristan liked to use when he was working on oil sketches, rather than using stretched canvas every time. The paintings were facing down, however, so she was unable to see them.

Put them back! Put the paintings back.

A wave of nausea swept over her, though she couldn't have explained why. Her fingers trembled, and the paper wobbled in response, but she still flipped it over.

Lara gasped.

The painting was beautiful, easily Tristan's best work.

A blonde woman reclined on a bed. She was naked, but there was nothing sexual about her pose. Instead, she appeared almost ethereal, her skin like cream and peaches, her hair silken strands of honey. It had the same quality of a Renaissance painting, only set in a modern era.

Amazed, Lara turned over the second painting. This one was of a different woman, but was just as good as the first, if not better. Her mouth fell open, and she checked the remaining paintings, too. They were of the same women and were all wonderful. These were even better than the paintings he'd done of her.

Something dawned on her. If he had these paintings, why was he so insistent on using hers for the gallery showing?

How long had he been painting other women? She didn't think it had been long, though it might have been that she'd only recently noticed his nocturnal antics. He had plenty of time to create more paintings for the exhibition, so why did he demand to use hers, though she'd made her feelings on how upsetting it would be for her perfectly clear.

A new emotion rose inside her. Anger. He'd deliberately hidden these new paintings and had painted them when he thought she'd been asleep. He'd always told her she was his muse, and that his art came from her as much as him. They were twins, he'd said, a part of one another. She couldn't possibly expect him to work without her.

Yet here was the proof that he was perfectly capable of creating his art without her involvement. She wanted to tell herself that the only reason he'd lied to her was because he was worried he'd hurt her feelings, but this was Tristan she was talking about. He'd already seen how upset she was at the thought of the exhibition, and he'd made her believe there was no other way. No other choice. He'd watched her cry and beg, had made her feel guilty for so much as suggesting that she get in the way of his dream, and all the while he'd known he was more than capable of painting someone other than her.

The truth of it hit her. He enjoyed her tears. He enjoyed this hold he had over her. He hadn't told her about the other paintings because that would have freed her.

Breathless with fury, she shoved the paintings back into the drawer and slotted it back down into the hidden compartment inside the radiator cover. Unable to bring herself to be in the studio for a moment longer, she stormed out, slamming the door shut behind her.

On the wall of the dining room, Tristan's prized painting of her hung as though in mockery of her.

She despised that painting. She loathed it so damned much, the hate curdled in her veins. Those silvery lines of stretch marks on her hips where she'd had a growth spurt at age fourteen, the red dots on her upper arms, the dimples on her thighs. He'd caught it all in such exquisite, disgusting detail.

Was it the painting she hated with such fury, or herself?

Barely thinking, she reached out to the kitchen knife block. She tightened her fingers around a metal handle, her knuckles white.

Lara shrieked in fury and lunged for the painting, sinking the blade into the canvas with cold satisfaction.

She wasn't thinking about the consequences of what Tristan would do when he saw the damage she'd caused. At that point, she didn't even care. This way, no one else would ever have to see the painting.

She cut and slashed, ragged knife marks across her frozen smile and ugly body, leaving a flap of her cheek hanging, and carving a chunk out of her belly and hip. She was blind with anger and emotion.

Something fluttered from the painting and landed at her feet.

She barely noticed, continuing her savage attack, but then the item was joined by another and another. At first, she thought they were pieces of the canvas she must have cut off, but then she saw how uniform in shape each of the items were.

Her anger drained from her and was replaced by confusion. The knife dropped from her fingers and clattered to the floor. She stared down at the rectangular pieces of paper at her feet. Not just one or two, but more than she could count, and yet more were protruding from the holes in the painting that she'd just cut. Rectangular in shape, on shiny, stiff paper. Were those photographs? Why on earth were there a whole heap of photographs in the back of the painting?

Still confused, Lara bent and picked one up. She turned it over. The photograph was of a naked woman sitting up in bed. She stooped and picked up another. This was a closeup of the woman's legs. Another was taken from behind, the curve of a buttock and lower back.

Lara didn't understand. Clearly, these were the photographs Tristan had used to create the paintings of the other women she'd found, but why had he hidden them in the back of her painting? And who were they? Was it something he was embarrassed about? Prostitutes, maybe? It didn't make any sense.

She scooped up another photograph. A different woman this time, but similar in looks. Opposite to her—blonde instead of dark, more like their mother's colouring. Was that why Tristan was embarrassed about having them? Because the women looked like their mother? Was it because they were naked? But Tristan had never had any problems with her being naked before, so why them? In fact, he was so unperturbed by it that he was happy to show it off to hundreds of people.

Holding the photograph closer to her face, she studied it. There was something similar about each of the photos that featured the women's faces—none of them made eye-contact with the camera. In fact, they seemed kind of slumped but were also strangely familiar...

Her blood ran cold, her heart seeming to stop in her chest.

The photographs dropped from her fingers and drifted to the floor. Lara staggered away from them.

No, no, no. That wasn't what she'd seen, was it? Bloodshot eyes. Staring.

The hair arranged around the throat, hiding any marks.

Lara let out a wail of despair and fell to her knees. She wanted to be wrong. *Had* to be wrong.

The women in the photographs were all dead.

Chapter Twenty-Nine

D espite her best efforts, no one tried to break into the house the previous night.

Erica had barely slept, startling awake at every noise. It was hard enough trying to sleep in a strange house, in a strange bed, without also being unable to switch off completely in case the killer made himself known. Her colleagues alternated the night shifts with whoever was working that day. They also needed to get some sleep after having spent their night in unmarked cars, watching the property for any sign of an intruder.

"It's early days yet," Carlton reassured her when they were back in the office. "We'd have been lucky to get a hit on the first night. Remember that he likes to plan."

"I know you're right." Something had been bugging her, however. "Can you go and question someone who works at the gallery? His name is Tristan Maher. He has a sister who goes there, as well. I don't know what it is about him, but he's been playing on my mind."

Carlton nodded. "Of course. I'll take Turner and go and speak with him."

"Thanks. Make it subtle. And obviously, if you see me and Rudd, you don't know us."

He did a mock salute. "Yes, ma'am."

That day, she and Rudd went back to the gallery and repeated what they'd done the day before, casually wandering around the wide open spaces, intermixing conversation about the paintings together with Erica talking about how it felt to now live alone. She'd dressed down, forgoing her usual suit for a woollen, boat-neck dress, tights and boots, wanting to appear smart without seeming formidable. Rudd had done the same. They were just two girlfriends out for the day, enjoying each other's company. They found excuses to talk to any male who seemed to be below the age of forty, making sure to throw in comments about Erica's newly discovered love of art since her husband had died. Plenty of the men had thrown them looks as though they thought Erica was hitting on them, and a couple had even asked for her phone number, which she'd refused to give. If she was right, whoever was responsible for murdering those women had their own way of finding out her personal details.

They didn't see either Tristan Maher or Carlton and Turner at the gallery, but that didn't mean anything. The place was vast, with multiple different rooms and areas.

Finally, when they could no longer spend any more time there without appearing suspicious, they returned to the office.

Turner and Carlton were already back.

"Did you speak to Maher?" she asked.

Carlton nodded. "Yes, we did. I'm not sure why he's caught your attention in particular. He has an alibi in the form of his sister for the nights the women were killed, and for the attack on Victoria Greg. He recognised their photographs but couldn't tell us anything more about them. He seemed concerned about the attacks and was happy to speak to us."

She pressed her fingers to her lips. "Hmm. I'm not sure what it was. Just the glare he gave me after I'd spilled coffee on his sister's jumper."

Carlton raised an eyebrow. "You can hardly expect him not to be pissed off for that."

"What about any injuries?" she asked. "Could you see any bruises on him?"

He shook his head. "Nothing obvious."

"We did the usual checks on his name," Shawn said, "to make sure he didn't have any arrests or cautions, and there was nothing in his background that gave us any cause for concern or any reason why we should suspect him any more than anyone else in the building."

"He's male," she pointed out, "and seems physically fit and strong. He'd have been able to climb onto the balcony or the back extension at Victoria Greg's place. Did you speak to Miss Greg, ask her if she knows him?"

"I took a photograph of him to the hospital to show her, but though she recognised him from working in the gallery café, she didn't point the finger at him being her attacker."

"Does she have any memory of the attack back yet?" Erica asked hopefully.

"No, not yet."

"So, it could have been him, she just doesn't remember."

Shawn shrugged. "That's not enough to do anything with."

Erica sighed. "I know. I'm probably wrong. Like you said, I can't blame the bloke for being annoyed at me for ruining his sister's top."

They'd interviewed a lot of men who worked at the Tate Modern. There was something about Maher, though, something that didn't sit right with her. She reminded herself of the number of young men who passed through the building every day, and how it could just as easily be any one of those as Maher.

All she could do was go back to the house that night and hope she and Rudd had said and done enough to lure the killer into the open.

Chapter Thirty

Tristan was going to know she'd found out. There was no way he couldn't. He knew exactly which painting he'd hidden the photographs inside of and would see that she'd destroyed it.

Lara tried to grasp some strands of hope, trying to make sense of it all. She didn't want to believe Tristan was responsible for killing those women. Could he really have broken into their homes during the night, murdered them, and then photographed the bodies? She found the paintings he'd done from the photos—that was what had made her so furious that she'd cut up her own portrait—but that didn't mean he'd been the one to do the killing, did it? He might have been working for someone else. This might be a commission, and Tristan hadn't even realised the women in the photographs were dead.

But then why all the secrecy—painting late at night when he thought she was asleep and then hiding the photos in the back of her painting? If there was an innocent explanation, he wouldn't have gone to all that trouble.

Plus, she *knew* Tristan. He was her twin. There had always been a part of her that was frightened of him. She remembered how cold he'd been after their parents had died. He'd shed tears when they'd been told and had done an impressive job of his voice breaking during their eulogy at their funeral, but it had been as though he'd been playing a part. The moment no one was looking, those tears dried right up, and before long, he'd been busy selling anything of their parents' that was worth something, that he didn't want to keep.

But killing women? Did she really think he was capable of that?

She remembered that day at Mrs Winthorpe's house, how she'd been so certain she'd find the old lady's body and the reason behind it. She'd thought Tristan had done something to her then, so she clearly *did* think he was capable of murder.

It dawned on her like a frost crystallising around her heart. Yes, she did.

Tristan was capable of killing those women, and if he was capable of killing them, then he could do the same to her.

He'd intended on showing the painting she'd destroyed. Had he imagined it on the wall of a gallery, knowing exactly what it contained within the mounting? Had it been because he'd thought it was better to hide them in plain sight, or was it because he'd got a kick out of the idea of so many people stopping to admire the picture, completely unaware of the horror behind the image?

Panic took over, and she scooped up the photographs, repulsed to be so close to them, while not knowing what else to do. A couple fell from her grasp and drifted to the floor again.

He would be back at any moment and see what she'd done. He'd know that *she* knew.

She needed to call the police.

Lara's heart pounded. If she called the police, they'd come here and arrest Tristan. Would the photographs be sufficient to charge him with the murders of those poor women? She didn't know exactly how it all worked, but would they be proof, or would they need something more—DNA evidence tying him to the scene? What if they arrested him then he got out and came after her to punish her for betraying him?

The possibility had her shaking with terror. He was already going to be furious when he saw what she'd done to one of his beloved paintings, but for her to then have called the police on him without even giving him a chance of explaining himself... well, it was something she doubted he would ever forgive her for.

And what if the police did arrest him and took him to prison and he was convicted and never got to come home again? Then she'd be all alone for the first time in her life, living in this house, all by herself. She'd been with Tristan since the moment of their conception and she'd never imagined having to live without him, even if she may have fantasised about it on the odd occasion.

Lara grew dizzy with the possibility, as though she was standing on the top of a tall building, her toes curled around the edges of the roof, looking down onto the vast drop below. But with the potential came a very real terror. What if she jumped and she just kept on falling? Or if she finally hit the bottom, not to land on her own two feet, but to become a bloodied smear on the pavement.

Still undecided, her head spinning, all she could think to do was gather up the photographs and pick up the destroyed painting. She'd hide it somewhere while she got her thoughts together and figured out what to do. She prayed he wouldn't notice right away, and it would buy her some time.

You're not buying yourself time. You're being a coward. You're not wanting to face up to what's real.

"No," she said. "I'm facing up to him. I'll ask him to tell me the truth. Then I'll know."

You're wasting time.

"Stop it! Stop it!"

She lifted both hands and battered herself on the head. She felt as though she'd woken up in a horror story. Her twin brother had murdered women, or if he hadn't done the killing, he was painting from photographs of murdered women. There were websites who dealt in this kind of thing, weren't there? Dark recesses of the internet where people could get access to all kind of depravity.

But she was sure these were the same women whose faces had been peering out at her from news sites and social media.

There was something else that bothered her. Each of them was blonde, they all had a similar kind of look, and they reminded her of someone.

They reminded her of their mother.

The room seemed to draw away at the edges, and Lara grasped for something to keep her upright. Passing out now would be a very bad thing indeed. Tristan would come home and find her unconscious, surrounded by his photographs and the ruined painting.

The thought gave her a jolt of adrenaline, bringing her back around. She needed to pull herself together.

Lara continued picking up the photographs and then the remains of the painting. She couldn't leave them down here. They might also be evidence, so she wasn't going to throw them away either. She carried them upstairs and into her bedroom where she shoved handfuls of the photographs under her mattress and then pushed the frame beneath her bed.

She felt better once they were out of sight, like she could think again. A part of her wanted to forget the past thirty minutes had ever happened and go back to not knowing.

Tristan wouldn't physically hurt her, would he? She was his twin. He'd scared her and he controlled and manipulated her, but he'd never actually laid a finger on her. She just needed to ask him some questions and then she'd know for sure. The moment she saw it in his eyes, she would phone the police.

The thought of handing her brother over to the police broke her heart. Even if he'd done the most terrible of things, that didn't stop her from loving him. He was a part of her, and they'd been together since the womb, but she couldn't let him carry on hurting women, if that was what he was doing.

Feeling as though she'd woken in a nightmare, she went downstairs and sat on the edge of the sofa, her hands clasped in her lap, waiting.

She had no idea how much time had passed since she'd been sitting there—hours, from the way her body was frozen in position and every muscle in her back ached—but finally the growl of an engine approached outside and then fell quiet. A car door slammed.

Oh God. He was home.

She grew dizzy with fear. She'd only been kidding herself when she'd thought he wouldn't notice the painting was no longer on the wall. Would he see in her eyes that she knew? No, she didn't know anything. Not really. She needed to give him the chance to explain himself. He wouldn't hurt her.

The sound of the front door opening and shutting drifted through to her, the clink of his keys hitting the hall console, the shuffle as he removed his coat and hung it up in the built-in cupboard under the stairs, and then kicked off his shoes. She memorised his routine down to the last second.

She knew him. She'd believed she knew everything about him. The possibility that she didn't know what her own twin was capable of was unthinkable.

With her breath held, she waited. He would have gone straight through to the kitchen-diner, then into the conservatory. Would he have noticed the missing painting yet? Had he spotted that she'd been in his studio?

"Lara?"

She froze, not knowing how to respond.

"Lara? Are you in? I saw your car outside."

"Yes," she called back, her voice tremulous. "I'm in here."

He still didn't bother to come into the room to speak to her. "I'm just heading up for a quick shower. Are you going to get dinner started?"

"In a minute."

He hadn't noticed, and she exhaled a long sigh of relief. But she couldn't pretend she hadn't seen anything, could she? What kind of coward would that make her if she put her head down and carried on like everything was normal?

Shakily, she got to her feet. Her stomach churned, and she felt weak, her bowels watery. She'd start making dinner and throw what she'd found casually into the conversation, and hope he'd give her a reasonable explanation for the photographs. If he did, she'd have nothing to worry about. He might be angry with her, but at least she wouldn't have to call the police. She could go back to thinking of Tristan as just being her brother.

She busied herself by opening the fridge and taking items out for dinner—prepacked minced meat, a packet of swollen, ripe tomatoes, some onions, and a bulb of fresh garlic. She placed them on the side—

A solid weight shoved her from behind, slamming her into the kitchen counter. She let out a gasp of shock, but before she could do anything, he'd grabbed her arms, yanked them behind her back, and secured her hands together with something hard and plastic that dug into her wrists.

"Tristan!" she cried.

He spun her around to face him. "What did you do with them?"

"What are you doing? You're frightening me."

"I know you found them. The painting is missing, Lara. Don't try to pretend you don't know."

"Maybe someone came into the house and took it?"

His laugh was cold. "Nice try."

She hadn't been planning on lying to him, but then she hadn't been expecting him to attack her either. She'd imagined they'd talk, and then she would make a decision. Not this.

"Please, Tristan. You're hurting my wrists."

"Your wrists? That's all you're worried about? Hasn't it registered with you what I'm capable of yet? You always were the stupid one. I swear, even when we were in the womb together, I fed from you. I got the brains, the looks, the strength. I took everything from you and I always have. Your only existence, Lara, is to make me stronger."

It was true. He'd weighed almost two pounds more than she had when they'd been born. Twins were often birthed earlier than single pregnancies, but in their case, the reason for the early caesarean was that the doctors had believed the female baby—Lara—would have died.

Fraternal twins don't share a placenta, and though technically Tristan couldn't have been taking anything from her in the womb, that didn't stop him from thinking he was the stronger twin. Stronger, and older, by a matter of seconds. That was something that had stayed with them both, not only through childhood, but into adulthood, too.

"Did you do it?" She had to know. "Did you hurt those women?"

"Yes, I did."

"Why? How could you?"

"Because I wanted to. I wanted to know how it would feel to create something all of my own."

"You didn't create anything!" she cried. "You destroyed things. You took those women's lives."

He snorted. "That's just your opinion. I created art. I took things of beauty and turned them into a form that would never grow old."

Lara shook her head, her mind spinning. "The photographs... they looked like Mum when she was younger."

"She was a slut."

It was insane, but his words shocked her almost as much as finding the photographs. "How can you say that!"

"Do you remember buying me that ancestry test for our birthday one year, and how I sent it off, but I told you the results never came back."

"Yes, I remember." It had been their seventeenth birthday. She'd thought it would be fun.

"The results *did* come back, I just never told you about them."

Her eyes filled with tears of confusion. "Why?"

"Here's the thing, Lara. You and I should share fifty percent of our DNA, just like any other brother and sister, except we don't."

"What are you talking about? We're twins. Of course we do."

"Except we don't. We only share twenty-five percent of our DNA."

Her head spun. "They must have got it wrong."

"They didn't. I checked."

"But... but how?"

"We're fraternal twins, which means, though we were born at the same time, we weren't necessarily conceived at the same time."

"What are you saying? That one of us was conceived at a different time to the other? But how would that affect our D—" She cut herself off as the reason sank in. "Oh."

A horrible smirk touched the corners of his mouth, his upper lip curling in disgust. "Like I said, our mother was a slut. She had sex with her husband *and* someone else within a week or so of each other. She conceived with both of them, and became pregnant with twins."

That was why she'd been smaller. It wasn't because he was the stronger twin. It was because she was most likely conceived later than he'd been, and they had different genes.

She almost didn't want to ask, but she had to. "Which of us is Dad's child?"

From the narrowing of his eyes and the hatred contained within them, he didn't even need to answer the question.

She was.

"Did... did you ask her, when she was alive? Did you ask her who your real father was?"

"No, I didn't want to give her the chance. More lies to come out of her dirty little whore mouth."

She knew him too well to know he wouldn't have just left it at that. "What did you do, Tristan?"

"I killed her, of course. Messed around with her seatbelt strap. Cut the brake fluid line. It all ended perfectly."

Her eyes filled with tears. "No, you couldn't have done that."

"I did." He shrugged, as though it was really no bother at all.

"But it wasn't only Mum who died, Dad did, too. What had he ever done to hurt you?"

"He was stupid and gullible. His wife having sex with another man right under his nose, and then him bringing up the child they'd conceived."

"You! He brought up you! You should have been thankful to him for that."

"He was a fool."

"How could you have expected him to know? Even I didn't know until this very moment. We're twins. What are the chances of that happening?"

"It doesn't matter to me. The most important thing is that I got what I wanted in the end. The house, their money, and you."

"You don't have me," she snapped.

He chuckled. "I think I do, Lara, darling. I always have. You're nothing without me."

"And you killed those women. Why? Because they reminded you of Mum? You were punishing her all over again."

"Maybe that was why those particular women caught my attention, but it was also for my art. You've seen those paintings, I know you have. They're some of my best work. And it was also just to see if I could. It was so easy, to take their lives. Snuff them out of existence in a matter of minutes."

Lara yanked at her wrists, trying to pull them apart, but whatever he'd tied them with held strong. "How could you?"

"I'm more than them. I'm more than any of you. I let them live on in my work. They'll never grow old or ugly. They'll always stay beautiful in my paintings. It's almost god-like, isn't it, to take a life and recreate it in your own form."

"You're insane."

"I still have more to do, sister dearest. I haven't decided what to do with you yet. And duty calls."

"No, Tristan! Please, don't hurt anyone else."

He grabbed her by the upper arm and dragged her through the house. She yanked back on him, trying to break free, but he was too strong. He reached the cupboard under the stairs and opened the door. One of her silk scarves hung from a peg—a purple one with black and white butterflies that he'd given her for Christmas one year—and he took it down and wrapped it over her mouth, so it pressed between her lips, and tied it at the back of her head. Then he threw her into the cupboard, and she fell down among the old shoes and coats, and the door slammed shut.

He was already gone.

Chapter Thirty-One

N ight had fallen once more.

Erica sat on the strange bed in the dark, her phone on the pillow beside her.

Waiting.

The previous day, she'd brought with her a small suitcase of toiletries and clothes, and so she'd changed out of the dress she'd worn during the day and had replaced the outfit with a pair of jogging bottoms and a long-sleeved t-shirt. If he was watching, she didn't want him to get any idea she was expecting him, but she also wanted to be wearing more than her usual vest and underwear to bed.

She took some comfort that Turner and Carlton were both parked in an unmarked car outside the front, keeping watch for any suspicious activity. If they saw anyone lurking around, they'd let her know right away. There were also two officers covering the rear. Gibbs had tried to convince her to have officers inside the property as well, but if the killer was watching the house, she didn't want him to think she had company. Part of his modus operandi was that the victim was always alone in the house when the attack happened, and she didn't want to risk putting him off because he'd seen others enter the property.

Her phone buzzed, and she snatched it up, her heart thudding. It was Shawn.

She kept her voice down, just in case, and spoke into the dark. "Yes?"

"Something's happened, Swift."

"What?" Had he seen something—someone?

"It's not what you think. We've just had a call come in that the body of another woman's been found. It's not far from here—about ten minutes away."

Her stomach dropped. "No!"

"I'm sorry, Swift. I know how much you wanted this to work."

Fuck! She'd been wrong. She wasn't sure which part she'd messed up on. Had she been wrong about the art gallery linking all the victims? Had she not made it obvious enough that she should be the next victim? Or had she been glaringly obvious and that had made him turn his attention elsewhere? Had her mistake got another innocent woman killed?

Erica was furious with herself.

"We think he might still be near the scene," Turner continued. "The woman doesn't look as though she's been dead long. The body is still warm, and neighbours reported hearing screams coming from the house only twenty minutes ago."

"Twenty minutes? Jesus Christ." She was already out of bed, jumping to her feet. "He can't have got far."

"That's what I was thinking. We're mobilising all police officers in the area to catch him, including those covering this house, so we're going to need you, too, I'm afraid."

It was a change in his modus operandi, the fact he'd attacked in the evening instead of the middle of the night. He was taking risks. People had heard him. There was a chance the victim had still been awake when he'd broken in and had called for help. He was getting reckless, and they needed to take advantage of that.

"That's fine. What's the address?"

Shawn rattled it off.

"Go," she instructed. "I'll meet you there."

"We can drive you."

"No, it'll waste time. I need to change and get my stuff together. Go, and I'll meet you there."

She ended the call.

From outside came the grumble of a car engine starting, followed by the glow of headlights and then the familiar flashing of the blue emergency lights and the rise and fall of the siren as they raced out of her road.

Erica quickly changed into her suit, zipped up her boots, and hurried from the bedroom. She ran downstairs and grabbed her car keys from the hall console and then plucked her heavy overcoat from where she'd hung it by the front door. It was cold out there tonight, and if they were going to be walking the streets, hunting down this killer, she was going to need the extra layer.

She stepped out of her front door, keys clutched in one hand, her phone in the other, and turned towards her car parked in the driveway.

Movement came from her right, something solid swinging towards her, colliding with her skull.

Darkness folded her into its arms.

Chapter Thirty-Two

E rica groaned and rolled to her back, wincing as pain shot through the side of her head. She blinked up at the night sky and shivered. It was freezing.

Was she outside?

No, she wasn't, she realised. Her view of the sky was through glass. She was inside but wasn't surrounded by solid walls. She was in a conservatory. There was a smell in the room, too, something powerful and bitter.

"You insulted me, DI Swift. Did you really think I was that stupid?"

The male voice snatched her attention, and she shifted onto her side, trying to get some understanding about what had happened. The shape of a man standing over her came into focus.

She recognised him instantly.

"Tristan Maher," she croaked. "What have you done?"

Her instincts had been right. He was the killer, and he'd not only taken another innocent life that night, she would most likely be next. She remembered his twin sister. Where was the young woman now? She'd said they lived together, hadn't she? Did the sister know what her brother was capable of? Was she involved somehow?

He shook his head at her, his lip curled in a sneer of disgust. "How could you think that I wouldn't be able to tell you were with the police? You took me for a mug?"

"No, I didn't think that," she said, though she didn't mean it. She had hoped he'd fall for it. In a way, he had. She knew who he was now. She just prayed she'd be able to tell someone else before he killed her.

She blinked and tried to sit up, but her hands were tied behind her back. Still, she wanted to get an idea of her surroundings, see if there was anything around that she could use to help her. She realised what the smell was—paint and solvent. She appeared to be in some kind of makeshift studio. All around her were artists easels displaying paintings.

Erica sucked in a breath.

The paintings were of all the other dead women, and pinned to the tops, were photographs he must have taken after he'd murdered them and then arranged their bodies.

So that's what you were doing? You were photographing them so you could paint them later.

The dead women weren't the only paintings on display. She also recognised those of his sister, though Erica assumed—and hoped—the other woman was still alive.

"I was one step ahead of you, DI Swift. Why else would I have killed that poor innocent young woman at this time? I wanted a commotion so that you'd be pulled away from your house, and the other police watching you would be distracted."

"You could have been caught."

He laughed. "But I wasn't, was I? And your people still have no idea who I am."

"Where's your sister? Is she dead, too?"

She was trying to buy herself time, trying to piece her thoughts together.

A muscle beside his eye twitched. "What?"

"You have a twin sister who you live with. I spoke with her as well. Where is she? Does she know what you do? Is she involved?"

"Leave her out of this."

She was a sore point, Erica could tell.

"What have you done with her?"

"Nothing. She just needed to be reminded of her place."

"You mean you've hurt her."

"No, I haven't. I would never hurt Lara. I've dedicated my life to looking after her."

"When the police catch up with you—and they will catch up with you—if she's been helping you in any way, she'll be prosecuted as well. Even if she didn't help kill those other women, if she covered up your crimes, she's complicit. She'll be charged as an accessory."

"She's not complicit. She had no idea what I was doing until today."

"She found out today? Why didn't she call the police then?"

"I stopped her."

Erica's mind raced. Was the other woman in the house with them? She wanted to know for sure.

"I'm sure you love your sister, Tristan. You must realise you're on borrowed time now. If she knows, she'll end up telling someone. What do you plan on doing? Keeping her a prisoner for the rest of her life."

He shook his head. "You're wrong. She won't tell."

"Then you will be making her complicit. You'll be responsible if she goes to prison for the crimes you've committed.

"Shut your mouth. I don't want to hear any more of your bullshit."

He drew back his foot and kicked her in the stomach.

The air exploded from her lungs, and she doubled over, pain radiating through her. She gasped for air and blinked back tears. For a moment, her mind went completely blank. All she could think of was the pain. But then it faded again, and she had to focus if she was going to get out of this alive. Was there anything nearby she could use as a weapon? If she was in a studio, there might be a palate knife or something. Through her tear-filled eyes and her position on the floor, she tried to look around, but nothing jumped out at her. She also had her hands tied behind her back, so even if she could get hold of something, she might not be able to use it.

How long had she been here for? She didn't think it had been long. He must have knocked her unconscious and thrown her into a car and brought her here.

Would Shawn and Carlton have realised what had happened to her? Would they be searching for her? She kicked herself for not telling the two other detectives to wait for her. They'd been parked right outside. But she'd been so aware of how every second counted when it came to catching a killer, and she hadn't wanted them to miss him just because they'd been waiting for her to find her boots and jacket.

"Do you know why you're still alive?" he asked, walking around her slowly, circling her body.

"Why?"

"Because I decided I didn't only want to paint from photographs any longer. I wanted to paint the real thing."

She allowed herself to experience a brief moment of hope. If he wanted to paint her, that would take time. How long did it take to finish a portrait—hours or days? She had no idea, but it would buy her time.

Then she realised what he really meant. She'd thought he was going to paint her while she was still alive, when he'd said that he wanted to paint her in real life. But he just meant he didn't want to paint her from a photograph.

He wanted to paint her dead.

Chapter Thirty-Three

There was someone else in the house.

Lara stopped her wriggling and listened hard. She'd been trying to get the scarf off her mouth and yank her hands from where they were bound behind her back, but nothing she did seemed to make any difference.

Tears slipped down her cheeks. She couldn't even start to put together everything she'd found out today. So many secrets.

Her brother, her twin brother. How could he have done this? He hadn't hurt her, only bound her hands and thrown her in here, but he'd hurt others. Their mother. Those poor women. How could she correlate her twin brother, the person she was closest to in her life, with that *monster*!

He wasn't even her twin anymore, not really. Though they'd shared a womb, they had different fathers. The idea left her shaken to her core. How could he have kept that secret from her all these years?

She was lying in the dark, among all their musty shoes, and damp coats, and boxes of random crap they'd collected over the years. The door was shut, but, unless he'd wedged a chair under the handle—something she hadn't heard him do—she didn't think it was locked.

A thin shaft of light came from the hallway outside, illuminating what was around her. She shuffled closer to the gap and listened again.

Yes, she could definitely hear voices. Tristan's and... was that a woman's voice?

Something twisted inside her. They never brought other people back to the house. In the eight years since their parents' deaths, she'd never known another person set foot inside their home. Why had that changed now?

Lara sat up again. She needed to get out of the damned cupboard. She reached out behind her with her joined hands and felt around.

Her fingers closed around smooth wood. It felt good in her palms, weighty.

What was that?

An idea occurred to her, and she wondered, even if she couldn't get the ties undone, maybe she could get her hands in front of her.

Lara wriggled back to sitting and pushed her hands close to the floor. Her shoulders strained, but she kept going, manoeuvring them down over her bottom, and then the backs of her thighs. She was practically folded in two, but she kept going, pulling her hands under her until she was finally able to thread her feet between her arms.

Her wrists were still tied, but at least now they were in front of her, and she was able to lift her hands to her face and yank down the scarf he'd tied around her mouth. She had to be cautious. Who did he have out there? While her instinct was to scream for help, she squashed it down. She didn't want to alert Tristan to her being free.

Slowly, she opened the cupboard door, and light flooded in.

She glanced behind her, remembering the item she'd touched. It was a baseball bat—like the type American's used.

Where had that come from? Sport definitely wasn't something Tristan had ever been into, and especially not American sport.

Lara bent and picked it up.

Chapter Thirty-Four

Erica yanked at the bindings on her hands, trying to use her body as a brace to snap them, but all it did was hurt, the plastic cutting painfully into her skin.

"Please, Tristan. You won't get time to paint me. My colleagues already know who you are, and they'll know I'm missing. They'll put two and two together and be here soon."

"They're too busy focusing on the other body," he scoffed. "I've got plenty of time yet. You'll be my greatest work of art."

A female voice came from the doorway leading into the rest of the house.

"You're painting her?"

Erica looked around. The diminutive figure of Tristan's twin sister stood in the doorway. She had a purple scarf around her neck, and her wrists were bound with a cable tie but were in front of her body.

There was something in her hands. Something long, and smooth, and wooden.

The baseball bat.

So, he *had* taken it from Victoria Greg's flat. Perhaps it was too late, but it was the physical proof they'd needed to link him to the attacks. Then she looked around at the photographs of the dead women and realised they no longer needed the bat to prove he was the killer.

"Lara, I'm a detective!" Erica cried. "Don't let him do this! Call the police."

"Behave yourself, Lara," Tristan snapped. "This isn't any of your business."

Lara's mouth dropped. "Not my business? You told me I was your muse. You were going to hang paintings of me in public, even when I begged you not to—"

His gaze darkened. "The painting you destroyed!"

She gave a laugh, and it sounded close to crazy. "You've *murdered* people. You killed our parents. I cut up a painting. I don't think you can compare the two.

"You don't have to live like this, Lara," Erica pleaded with her. "You can change things."

Her gaze flicked to Erica, as though she'd only just remembered the other woman was there.

Erica widened her eyes at the bat, trying to tell her to use it, but Lara barely seemed aware that she had it in her hand.

"These women became a part of my art," he said, still addressing his sister. "I'm not just an artist, I'm an artisan. Murder is my craft. But I'd never have hurt you, Lara. You know that, don't you? I painted you because I loved you."

Erica kept trying. "Don't let him do this, Lara. You're your own person. You're more than just his sister."

She stood there, her eyes wide with fright, frozen with indecision.

Tristan spun to Erica. "I need to shut you up for good."

He approached her, each step bringing him closer. Erica kicked out, lifting her knees to try to block him, but it did no good. He was strong and flattened her legs with his body weight, climbing on top of her.

"Lara, please!" she cried, hating the panic in her voice. "The police will look after you. You don't have to be an accessory to your brother's life anymore."

Tristan's eyes were blank, devoid of any emotion. Erica threw herself from side to side, trying to dislodge him, but nothing helped. His hands wrapped around her throat, his fingers cold and hard, and he squeezed. The air cut off from her lungs, and though she tried desperately to inhale, only a wheezing sound came from her lips.

His body had blocked her view of his sister, but Erica knew she was still there. Would she really do nothing and watch her brother kill someone?

Help me, Lara!

Tristan stared down at her, directly into her eyes, as though trying to imprint every second of this onto his mind. It was as though he wanted to pinpoint the exact moment the life went out of her. Her vision grew misty and blurred at the edges. Surely, this wasn't going to be how it all ended. How would Poppy live without her?

A tantalising voice sounded in her head... *Poppy will be fine. Natasha will take care of her. You can be with Chris again...*

No, she didn't want to give up! Her daughter needed her.

A sudden swing of movement and air came from above her, followed by a resounding crack. Then the hands were gone from her throat, and Tristan toppled sideways, collapsing on the floor beside her.

Standing above her was Lara, the baseball bat still clutched in her bound hands.

Erica rolled to her side, away from Tristan, gasping for air and coughing as oxygen rushed into her lungs.

Lara dropped to a crouch beside her, the baseball bat clattering to the floor. "I'm sorry. I'm so sorry. Are you okay?"

"Call nine-nine-nine," Erica managed to say between coughing fits.

Lara nodded and rose to standing.

Erica thought again. "No, wait. Untie me first."

Lara hurried back into the kitchen and returned with a pair of scissors. Erica didn't take her eyes off Tristan, praying he'd stay down, as Lara cut the cable tie. Erica rubbed her wrists, thankful to be free, and then did the same for Lara.

"Where's your phone?" Erica asked.

Lara pointed to a desk in the corner.

Erica hurried over, lifted the handset, and punched in Shawn's number.

Chapter Thirty-Five

Tristan Maher was starting to regain consciousness, though the back of his head and hair was matted with blood from where his sister had struck him with the baseball bat.

Erica took pleasure in clipping handcuffs onto the bastard's wrists.

He let out a groan and tried to sit up. "Get off me."

She pushed him back down. "Not a chance. Tristan Maher, you are under arrest for the murders of Kerry Norris, Emma Wilcox, and the attempted murder of Victoria Greg. You are also being charged with the abduction and attempted murder of a police officer, and for the murder of Norah Crawford."

Erica had only just learned the name of the third murdered woman—the thirty-year-old he'd killed before her abduction—and her heart tightened with sorrow as she said the words. There wasn't supposed to have been any more deaths, but she'd failed at that.

"I'll take it from here," Carlton said, taking hold of Maher's upper arm and hauling him out of the house, towards the waiting patrol car. "You need to get checked over by the paramedics."

"I'm fine, Carlton."

He threw her a stern look. "Get that head injury checked out."

"Okay, okay. I will, I promise."

Shawn and Carlton had arrived, together with several squad cars filled with uniformed police, within ten minutes of her making the call. She didn't think she'd ever been so happy to see them.

She turned to where Lara sat on a chair at the dining room table, her expression stunned, and face pale.

"You did the right thing," she said to the other woman. "Thank you."

Lara Maher nodded, though she didn't appear convinced. Erica thought that poor Lara was going to need some serious counselling in the weeks and months to come. She was going to have to rethink her entire adult life.

Shawn approached, his expression stern.

"Are you going to nag me as well?" she teased him. "I already told Carlton I'll let the paramedics check me over."

Truth was, her throat hurt almost as much as where she'd been hit across the head, and when she spoke, her voice sounded raspy. She thought she'd have bruises for at least a week.

He didn't smile. "Erica, you need to call your sister."

Her stomach flipped, and the smile fell from her face. "Natasha? Why?" That had been the last thing she'd expected to hear. "Is everything all right? Is it Poppy?"

"Poppy's fine," he assured her, "but you still need to call her."

Natasha was probably going to nag her again that she still hadn't managed to visit Dad. She wished her sister understood how important her job was and that she wasn't just doing this for a laugh. She might not be a brain surgeon or a scientist discovering a cure for cancer, but she was still saving lives. Maybe her plan hadn't panned out quite as she'd anticipated, and it broke her heart that another innocent woman had died, but at least he'd been stopped.

There would be no more killings.

There would most likely be a trial, of course, but with the amount of evidence at the property, there was little chance of Tristan Maher not going down for a very long time.

Shawn handed Erica his phone—hers had been lost at some point after Tristan had hit her—and she used it to call her sister before stepping away from the busy hubbub of the house.

Natasha answered on the first ring.

"'Rica?"

Immediately alarm shot through her. Rica was the name her sister had always called her when they'd been children.

"Tash? What's wrong?"

"Dad's dead." Her voice crumpled, and she choked back hitching sobs.

Erica didn't compute the words. "What?" She must have misheard. Her sister hadn't just told her their dad was dead.

"Are you there, 'Rica? Did you hear me?"

She forced herself to turn her attention back to the call. "Yes, I'm here."

"Dad's dead, Erica. He died tonight."

Her legs folded, and she sat down heavily. "How?"

She felt like she'd been punched in the chest, numb and disbelieving. That couldn't be right. He'd been doing better. They'd all told her so.

"I'm not sure. They think maybe a stroke, but they don't know for sure. He just died. He just gave up and died." Her voice broke on a sob.

Erica clamped her hand over her mouth. "Oh God. Not Dad."

The events of the past twenty-four hours suddenly didn't feel real. Like she had two different versions of reality. While she'd been caught up with a killer, her dad had been dying, and she'd never even had the chance to say goodbye.

• • • •

PEOPLE SAID FUNERALS weren't the place for children, but it had felt right to Erica that Poppy had the chance to say goodbye to her granddad just as much as she needed the chance to say goodbye to her dad. Otherwise, in Poppy's mind, the funeral might become something dark and hidden in grownup secrets, rather than simply a time for them to reminisce, shed a few tears, sing some songs, and put Frank Haswell's body to rest.

The family perched on the hard, dark wooden pews at the front of the church. Both of Natasha's older children were also here, being brave and taking care of their younger cousin. The baby was too young to understand, and one of Natasha's friends who also had a child of the same age had offered to have her for the day. Natasha sat, holding her husband's hand tightly, her head bent in sorrow.

The coffin was at the front, with displays of lilies positioned on either side. The vicar and both of Frank's daughters had welcomed most people at the church gate as they had arrived, shaking hands and doing their best to smile. Everyone spoke in low, muted tones, and though they'd said in the funeral announcement that people should wear bright colours to celebrate Frank Haswell's life, plenty of people had still shown up in black. Many of the staff from Willow Glade Care Home were there, too, and she exchanged a grateful smile with Monica. There were some other distant relatives who'd come to the funeral—a second cousin and some other elderly people who were most likely not actually joined by blood, but who thought of themselves as cousins.

Erica glanced behind her and spotted Shawn slipping into one of the pews at the back. He looked handsome in his dark-grey suit, and he caught her eye and gave her a sympathetic nod and a smile. Her heart warmed at his presence. It meant a lot that he'd come. There were other ex-members of the Met, too, police officers and ex-detectives who'd known Frank Haswell when he'd been in the force.

The vicar stood at the front of the church, and everyone fell quiet. He welcomed the congregation and said a few words about Frank, and then they sang a hymn.

Erica pushed down her nerves and got up to speak, taking her place in the small pulpit, to look into the faces of all the people who'd turned out to remember her dad.

"Thank you, everyone, for coming to help celebrate our dad's life. Frank Haswell was the best kind of man." She struggled to speak against the painful lump constricting her throat. "He was strong, and sensible, and kind, and he never liked a fuss about anything." She raised a teary smile. "Honestly, he probably would have hated all of this."

Her words got a ripple of laughter from the pews, the sense of relief at the break in the tension palpable.

"As many of you know, I lost my husband not so long ago, and to now lose the other man in my life is harder than I could ever imagine. But even though we lost Dad in one of the cruellest ways through his dementia, I'm so grateful that we got so many years with him. He was a wonderful dad, and a fantastic husband, though I'm sure Mum would have had something to add to that if she was still alive..." More laughter rose from the pews. "He inspired me to become the person I am today, and I will miss him more than I can ever put into words."

Tears threatened to bubble up, and she covered her mouth with her hand. Fingers pressed to her shoulder, and she looked over to see her sister had left the pew and was now standing beside her.

Natasha nodded to the seat she'd just left. "I'll take it from here."

The rest of the service went smoothly, and when it was time for everyone to leave, the unmistakable opening guitar riffs of *Don't Fear the Reaper* by Blue Oyster Cult started up and made everyone laugh again. Her dad would have smiled at the inappropriateness of it.

Later, in the churchyard, she and Natasha found a moment to be alone.

"He was proud of you, you know," Natasha said. "So much prouder than he ever was of me."

"That's not true, Tash."

Natasha nodded and smiled sadly. "It's true."

"But you were there for him in his final days when I was caught up in work."

"He would have understood. You know he would." Natasha took her hand and gave it a squeeze. "Do you think he's with Mum now?"

"I hope so, but you know I'm not a believer in all that stuff."

Erica remembered her thoughts as Tristan Maher's hands had been around her throat, how she'd believed she would be with Chris in death, and wondered how much she could get behind her own words.

"It's okay," Natasha continued, "I can believe for the both of us. I think it's where he'd want to be the most. You know how often he asked after her, how he always called the both of us Yvonne. Maybe he always knew he was going back to her one day and he was just preparing himself for that."

"You think Mum's ready for him?" she said with a teary smile. "She might have been enjoying the peace and quiet."

"I'm sure she was ready for him. I bet they're back together again, and Mum is healthy and Dad's got his memory back, and now they're going to live that retirement they never got the chance to enjoy."

Erica liked hearing her sister's version of things, and she hoped that was true. Maybe Chris was with them? No, she shut that thought down with a rueful internal smile. Chris had been brilliant with her dad when he'd been living with them, but she was fairly sure hanging out with her parents for the whole of eternity would have been Chris's idea of hell.

"What are you smiling about?" Natasha asked her.

"Oh, nothing. Just picturing Mum and Dad together again, that's all."

Erica had deliberately done what she could to keep the truth of what had happened with Tristan Maher away from her sister. Natasha had warned her that it would be dangerous, and that she was putting her family in jeopardy as well, and Erica didn't want to be told that Natasha had been right. Erica had simply told Natasha that things hadn't gone to plan and he'd tragically murdered another woman, and then he'd been later apprehended at his house. She hoped the press weren't going to get hold of the full details of what had happened—though they normally didn't care who caught the killer, only that the case was solved—or she'd end up having to answer some awkward questions from her sister. She already knew there were going to be plenty of those in the weeks and months to come.

"Come on," Natasha said, tugging her down the church path, towards the waiting guests. "Let's go and drink to Dad."

Erica smiled, and a tear slipped down her cheek. "Yes, he would have liked that."

Acknowledgements

I couldn't write these books if it wasn't for the amazing team of people I have supporting me. Even though I always feel a bit like I'm repeating myself in these passages, I can't not show my gratitude to everyone who helps bring one of my books to life.

Thank you to my editor, Emmy Ellis, for accommodating my sudden change of dates! If you haven't come across Emmy Ellis's crime books yet, and you love your crime with a good measure of twisted gore thrown in, then you must go and search for her on Amazon.

Thanks to Patrick O'Donnell for consulting with me on the aspects of police procedural once again. I put off writing crime for a long time before I was always terrified of getting it wrong, and you've helped build my confidence no end.

Thank you to my proofreaders, Tammy Payne, Jacqueline Beard, and Glynis Elliott. I always appreciate your keen eyes when it comes to seeing what I can't!

And finally thank you to Mel Comley for her unwavering support and everyone in her reader group for reading and reviewing. Those reviews make the world of difference to me.

And as always, a huge shout of thanks to you, the reader, for keeping my dream of writing alive. I hope to never disappoint you.

Until next time!

M K Farrar

About the Author

M K Farrar is the pen name for a USA Today Bestselling author of more than thirty novels. Though 'Some They Lie' was her first psychological thriller, it wasn't her last, and she's now written eight novels of crime and psychological fiction. When she's not writing, M.K. is rescuing animals from far off places, binge watching shows on Netflix, or reading. She lives in the English countryside with her husband, three daughters, and menagerie of pets.

You can sign up to MK's newsletter at her website, mkfarrar.com. She can be also be emailed at mkfarrar@hotmail.com. She loves to hear from readers!

Also by the Author

Crime after Crime series, written with M A Comley

Watching Over Me: Crime after Crime, Book One

Down to Sleep: Crime after Crime, Book Two

If I Should Die: Crime after Crime, Book Three

Standalone Psychological Thrillers

Some They Lie

On His Grave

In the Woods